COPPER
and
GOLDIE

13 Tails (Short Stories) of Mystery and Suspense in Hawai'i

By
Rosemary and Larry Mild

Magic Island Literary Works • Honolulu, Hawai'i • 2019

Individual short stories appearing in *Copper and Goldie, 13 Tails of Mystery and Suspense in Hawai'i,* originally appeared in the following issues of *Mysterical-E:*

"Locked In: The Beginning," January 2015
"A Dead Man Isn't Fare," April 2015
"Death by the Pixel," July 2015
"The Getaway Cab," Fall 2015
"The Kidnapped Youngster," Fall 2016
"High Stakes in Honolulu," Winter 2016
"A Walk in the Dark," Summer 2017
"Carnival Caper," Spring 2018
"Peggy and Goldie," Fall 2018

"The Snake Lady" was published in *Dark Paradise: Mysteries in the Land of Aloha* (Anthology, 2017). All stories are reprinted by permission.

Interior book design by **Larry Mild**.
Cover design by **Marilyn Drea**, Mac-In-Town, Annapolis, MD.

Library of Congress Cataloging-in-Publication Data
Mild, Rosemary P. ; Mild, Larry M.
Copper and Goldie, 13 Tails of Mystery and Suspense in Hawai'i
Mild, Rosemary P. ; Mild, Larry M.

ISBN 978-0-9905472-5-9
First Edition 2019
10 9 8 7 6 5 4 3 2 1

Dedication

For our beloved grandchildren—
Alena, Craig, Ben, Leah, and Emily

For our wonderful children—
Jackie and Myrna

For our marriage—
Soul mates, partners, lovers

Acknowledgments

We could fill an entire volume with the names of all the family members, dear friends, and acquaintances who are loyal fans of our books, essays, and short stories. And you, our readers, are all precious to us and give us the ultimate push to continue our writing. **Our special thanks and hugs to:**

Joe DeMarco, Editor of *Mysterical-E,* online mystery magazine, for his enthusiasm in publishing nine "Copper and Goldie" short stories.

Sisters in Crime/Hawai'i Chapter and **Hawai'i Fiction Writers,** for their friendship, encouragement, and advice.

Marilyn Drea, our superb graphic artist, for her excellent covers.

Cliff and Nancy Halevi, for allowing us to include photos of Tavi, their wonderful golden retriever.

Laurie Hanan, our friend and fellow author, for her expertise on the Hawai'ian language.

Diane Farkas, our close friend, for her outstanding proofreading skills.

Susan Saul, our cousin and master jeweler, for the photo of her beautiful snake ring (p. 156). It's one of the "Artful Adornments" that Susan creates for her own company, Susan Saul: Jewelry and Metalsmithing. We discovered the snake ring on her website and were inspired to incorporate it in "The Snake Lady" as a flamboyant, important clue to catching the villain.
www.susansauldesign.com

Disclaimer

Copper and Goldie, 13 Tails of Mystery and Suspense in Hawai'i is a work of fiction. The plots and events therein are of the authors' imagination and invention. All characters therein are fictitious and any resemblance to persons living or dead is purely coincidental. A few locations have been altered to accommodate the stories.

Woof! I'm Tavi, Goldie's understudy and role model.

ABOUT TAVI AND GOLDIE

WOOF! MY NAME IS TAVI AND I BELONG TO CLIFF AND Nancy Halevi, who live in Kailua, on the island of O'ahu. I'm also the happy granddog of Lynne Halevi, Cliff's mom (and close friend of authors Rosemary and Larry). It is with the Halevi family's permission that my photographs appear in *Copper and Goldie, 13 Tails of Mystery and Suspense in Hawai'i* (on the front cover; and on pages vi, 50, 81, and 177). "Tavi" is Hebrew, from the Aramaic meaning "good," and I'm a good boy! My admiration of Goldie Nahoe is making me a celebrity in the canine world. If I could read, she would be my favorite character. Don't tell anyone, but I could do all of Goldie's tricks and stunts. And guess what! You can follow me on Instagram at HawaiianRetriever.

You see, I'm a golden retriever. Goldens are Scottish gun dogs that can be trained to hunt and do field work. There isn't a mean bone in all of our breed. In fact, you'll rarely find one of our fluffy, furry kind without a smile. Because of this unique trait, the authors of this book had to conjure up a dollop of Doberman (guard dog) blood for Goldie to help Sam catch bad guys and gals.

By the way, these authors do know that a tail is something that follows me around wherever I go, and a tale is a story told about a dog like me. Rosemary grew up with a golden named September Blaze. She devotes a chapter to him in her memoir *Love, Laugh, Panic! Life with My Mother*. Rosemary and Larry also immortalize a golden in *Locks and Cream Cheese*, their first mystery novel, where Shana helps catch a vicious thug. Shana is owned by a psychoanalyst, patterned after Rosemary's father, who—in real life—owned three rescue goldens: Oedipus Rex, Jerome, and Gus. So now you see why I'm so fond of these authors.

§

vii

Copper and Goldie
13 Tails of Mystery and Suspense in Hawai'i

Table of Contents

Locked In: The Beginning

TODAY SAM NAHOE CAUGHT HIS THIRD MAJOR CASE SINCE making detective sergeant in the Homicide unit of the Honolulu Police Department. He now wore a gold badge instead of a silver one.

Sam and his partner, Corporal Mose Kauahi, hurried over to a mid-rise apartment house at 2330 Lanahi Place. The call came in at 9:30 a.m. The caller said she'd been trying to phone her neighbor for several days without a response. As a last resort, she went outside and peeked in his first-floor window. She saw him collapsed over his desk.

The detectives met the woman inside the apartment lobby. Sam's keen eyes assessed her. Waist-length kinky blonde hair, dark at the roots. Fortyish trying to look thirty, and less businesslike than he expected in a lacy pink tank top and short shorts.

She flashed Sam a heavily lipsticked smile. "I'm Doris Haliburton. You can call me Doris."

Jeez, the broad is actually flirting with me, thought Sam without missing a step.

They followed her down the hall to apartment 1A. Sam tried the door and found it locked. "It's another one of those steel security doors with anti-pick locks," he announced. "We'll have to find another way in. Is there a resident manager here?"

Doris shrugged. "Only part-time. But I s'pose you could try the windows out back." Without waiting for consent, she started down the hall. Sam couldn't help but notice the smooth legs, looking decades younger than her sun-creased face. At the rear of the building she held the door open for both men, an exit to a fenced-in backyard. "It's those two double windows—there and there—the ones on the left," she pointed. Her voice quavered. "He's in the living room."

Sam frowned. "Those windows are pretty high. You look to be about five-two. How could you see in?"

"I used my kitchen stool," Doris answered smugly.

Mose stepped closer. "It would be helpful if we could use it too," he said. "That is, if you wouldn't mind, ma'am."

She flinched at the word "ma'am." Sam knew why. It made women feel old.

"Yeah, sure, I'll get it. I'm in apartment 1C. Back in two shakes."

Mose had no intention of letting Doris out of his sight. He followed her inside, and the two returned with him carrying the stepstool. He placed it below the first set of double windows. The short, stocky detective climbed up only to find that he couldn't see much past the window sill. He yielded to Sam. Nearly a head taller at six-four, Sam climbed up until he had a clear view into what was obviously the living room. It was furnished with two leather couches, a glass-topped coffee table, and an elaborate entertainment center on the left wall. *A rather affluent bachelor pad*, he guessed. But in the far right corner against the wall, sure enough, a man's body lay slumped over a large modern desk.

Sam examined both double windows leading to the living room for signs of forced entry, but found none. He tried to at least jiggle each section, but each one was immovable, locked in place, with self-locking dowels to the right and left. He climbed down and moved the stepstool to the second set of double windows, hoping for better luck. Climbing back up, he peered into a bedroom and tested that set of windows with the same result. He decided entry there would cause less damage than in the more elegant living room.

"We'll have to get a locksmith for the front door," said Mose.

"Can't wait for that. The man may need medical attention," replied Sam. He removed a pair of sunglasses from his forest-green sport shirt and handed them down to Mose while he mulled over the best way to enter. The Venetian blinds were raised to their full height, so he wouldn't have to deal with them. Removing his Glock 9mm from its holster, he turned his head away, and ducked to his left as he drove the weapon, handle first, against the lower glass panel, cracking it sharply away from him so that the shards fell inside the room and dropped to the floor. He swept the barrel of his gun back and forth to remove the remaining shards from the frame. Reaching through the cleared opening, he released the pair of locks from their side stops, and slid the tall window all the way up.

"Hey, Mose, would you get me the floor mats from the front of the cruiser?"

When his partner returned with the mats, Sam dropped them over the concentration of glass shards inside the window.

He cautiously planted his size-thirteen shoes on the top step of the stool, then wiggled his backside onto the window ledge. Lifting one leg at a time over the sill, he slid inside. He landed for a split-second on his feet, but his muscular bulk gave way, sending him flopping on his knees. He heard, and felt, the crunching of the shards beneath the floor mats as he landed. Hoisting himself to his feet, he surveyed his surroundings. He had landed next to a queen-size bed with a quilted headboard and plaid comforter. He saw nothing out of order in the room; only an uncluttered bureau and nightstand.

The moment Sam entered the living room, the stench of decay hit him. He whipped out a handkerchief from his back pocket and covered his nose and mouth.

The motionless body slumped over the desk was a male of

3

medium build, narrow-shouldered, wearing a muted-print aloha shirt. He appeared to have been working on his laptop. His head of thinning sand-colored hair lay face-down on the keyboard. The monitor reflected the impact with a string of unintelligible letters and numbers. On the desk he saw documents and spreadsheets in neat piles; nothing else but a tape dispenser and vinyl cup holding ballpoint pens. The printer on the left corner of the desk contained no printouts. Sam leaned over, and with his free hand placed two fingers on the victim's carotid artery, feeling for signs of life. There was no pulse. But he knew there wouldn't be. In the middle of the man's back he found two bullet holes, close together, with accompanying patches of dried blood, obscuring the shirt's flowered pattern. He hastily backed up when he realized he had almost stepped in blood that had dried on the plush beige carpet. They had themselves a crime scene.

"We've got a stiff here, Mose," Sam called out. "Male, maybe fifty. Shot in the back, two small-caliber wounds. Dead a couple days, I'd say, from the smell of things. No weapon. We can't touch anything. We have to call the crime scene bunch. Come around front through the lobby. I'll let you in."

Pulling on a pair of Latex gloves, Sam tried to open the door of apartment 1A to go out into the hall. But in addition to the anti-pick lock, he discovered a second lock—keyless—with a rectangular-shaped deadbolt operated by only an inside thumb-latch. *Deadlocked from the inside,* he determined. *No way anybody broke into this door.* He turned the thumb-latch, then the doorknob, and let Mose in.

Without invitation, Doris slipped in behind Mose. Sam noticed that she seemed to know her way around. She scooted across the room and plopped herself into the La-Z-Boy recliner that sat about ten feet from a large flat-screen TV. But the rotten odors of death permeated the air. She wrinkled her nose in disgust, jumped up, and darted back out to the lobby.

Mose also reacted to the smell, pulled out his checkered handkerchief, and covered his face. Pecking away at his cell phone, he delivered the necessary report to their lieutenant in Homicide. The detectives left the apartment door slightly ajar so they wouldn't get locked out and retreated to the lobby to wait for the Crime Scene Investigation team.

In the lobby Doris sat huddled in an upholstered chair, her mop of hair almost hiding her face. While they waited for CSI, the detectives questioned her. She looked up at them, teary-eyed and sniffling. Moist mascara smudges dotted her sharp cheekbones.

"I still can't believe he's dead," she said, her face a mixture of distress and horror. "His name is, I mean was, James Castile." She explained that he was a department manager at one of the anchor stores at the Ala Moana mall. "He was a pleasant fellow—wouldn't hurt a soul. A nice man. No living relatives that I know of."

"How well did you know him?" Sam asked.

She hesitated. "We…had a few dates."

"How many?" Sam asked. He noticed her eyes had shifted to one side.

"Well, about a dozen."

"Do you have any idea why anyone would want to kill him?"

She shook her head. "No—except maybe that he liked to gamble some."

"Some?"

A scowl approaching anger crossed her face. "He played online poker. A lot."

She turned silent, pressing her lips together, creating worry lines that emanated from the corners of her mouth.

Sam persisted. "Did he owe you money?"

She shrugged. "Some."

Between the shifting eyes and the "some" he saw a practiced evasive manner and decided to keep his approach formal.

"Just how much, Miss Haliburton?"

Her ash-gray eyes smoldered. "About $4,000."

The detectives looked at each other.

* * * *

By 12:30 p.m., the CSI unit had finished their routine evidence search. No prints, no fibers. Nothing useful. They were not pleased that the bedroom window had been smashed, wondering whether evidence had been destroyed. Sam owned up to breaking it and explained there was no other way to enter the apartment, but he assured them he had disturbed nothing. The investigators placed a sheet of clear plastic over the gap, as well as crisscrossed yellow crime-scene tape. After the necessary crime scene photographs, the body was transported to the morgue.

What bothered Sam most was the lack of access to this first-floor corner apartment. It nagged at him until his gaze settled on the living room windows facing the rear of the building. They were fairly well concealed from the next apartment building by thick hibiscus bushes. He speculated that the killer shot Castile, locked both doors from the inside, and let himself out through one of the self-locking windows. He had to be wearing gloves because he'd left no prints.

Sam tried slipping the window frame up while pulling in the two spring-loaded dowels from the anti-theft stop holes on both sides. He discovered that they had to be re-pulled every four inches from fully open to fully closed—a whole new problem. How could the perpetrator pull the dowels while he was dropping to the ground? He'd have to be double jointed. Until Sam examined the stop holes on the opposite window he was totally stymied.

There he discovered that strips of Scotch tape had been laid in the tracks, covering all the stop holes except for the last pair, which allowed the panel to lock in its frame as the killer left the scene. The exposed side of the strips appeared to be wiped clean, and any unlikely prints on the opposite or sticky side would probably be destroyed during removal. The killer must have taken the Scotch tape off the dispenser on the desk. The CSI team would have dusted the dispenser, but maybe the tape itself had something to offer. He went back to the desk, picked up the dispenser, and forced a breath of air over the tape. Sure enough, a single print emerged. The killer must have removed his gloves to manipulate

6

it.

"Mose, get an evidence bag from the car trunk, please. I think we've got a clear print here." Sam also made a mental note to retrieve their floor mats from the bedroom.

* * * *

At 10:30 the next morning the report came back from the FBI's Automated Fingerprint Identification System (AFIS). It revealed a twenty-four-point match—to a woman! Daisy Skinner, aka Doris Skinner, aka Doris Haliburton, a skilled con artist wanted in several states. Sam and his partner went to pick her up. Mose rang the bell next to her nameplate. It took four rings before she answered the intercom and buzzed them in. She stood in her doorway in jeans and a bulky University of Hawai'i Warriors sweatshirt—a far cry from her coquettish outfit of the day before.

"Sorry I took so long. I was indisposed," she murmured in a throaty voice, batting her lashes thick with fresh mascara. "You know how that is, gentlemen. Come on in. How can I help you?"

Sam felt the woman's eyes scan him—from his curly black hair to his broad chest and arms, like he was something to be devoured. He had three-quarters Hawai'ian blood and a *haole* (Caucasian) maternal grandmother, all of which accounted for his charisma. Women were drawn not just to his physique, but to his strong square jaw, ruddy complexion, and high, round cheekbones that hinted of Polynesian ancestry.

But he saw through Doris—she was only flirting to distract him. He nodded briefly, shrugging off the unwanted attention, and stepped past her. Mose followed.

Inside her apartment, Sam immediately got the impression of an exceptionally well-heeled tenant. Living room with teal-blue wall-to-wall carpeting; tweed sofa with matching side chairs; full kitchen with gleaming appliances. An open door revealed a spacious bedroom with a four-poster bed. The black-lacquered nightstand held a stack of books. The title of the one on top read *Online Texas Hold'em Poker.*

"Doris Haliburton," Sam announced, "you are under arrest

for the murder of James Castile." He began reciting her Miranda rights. As he was about to cuff her, she pivoted and faced him. "Detective," she said with a Marilyn Monroe breathiness, "I assure you this is all a terrible misunderstanding. I couldn't even get inside his apartment, let alone murder the poor man."

"Look, lady," Mose interjected. "We got your prints on the Scotch tape."

"You've got to be kidding me. How is that relevant, Detective?"

"It was obvious," said Sam. "Our perpetrator had to be the last person to use the dispenser. You used tape to block the window stops. You needed it for your retreat from the crime scene."

"But gentlemen, if I killed him he couldn't very well pay me back, could he? After all, he owed me a bundle." She smiled with the satisfaction of her logic.

"Miss Haliburton, I agree," said Sam. "I'm thinking it's the other way around. You're the gambler, the big loser. But you have expensive tastes. You borrowed the money from him and didn't want to pay it back. We can easily check that out."

She shrugged. "So what?" Her smile remained fixed, but her eyes turned cold. "Can I get my purse from over there on the table?"

"Sure," said Mose, "after I look through it first." He opened the Coach handbag of soft leather and dumped out the contents, when he heard a harsh voice behind him.

"Is this what you're looking for?" Doris held a .22-caliber target pistol pointed straight at him. She had hidden it under her sweatshirt, tucked into her jeans belt.

Just as he heard the click of the gun's safety, Sam dove to knock Mose out of the line of fire. He heard the shot and felt a sting in his back—just as the bullet lodged in his spinal cord channel. Mose hit the floor first. Sam fell almost on top of him.

Mose rolled free in one rapid move, pulled out his weapon, and managed to fire three quick shots angled from the floor at the fleeing Doris Haliburton. The first shot blew out the back of her right knee, the second went through the main leg artery, and the third landed upward, deep into her chest. She screamed twice, convulsed, and died.

* * * *

Mose, grateful for his own life, used his cell phone to call an ambulance to the scene. He turned pale when he saw his partner in agony on the floor. Sam was still alive, but suffering from pain and shock. By noon he lay on his stomach on the operating table. But there were hard choices to be made. The doctors had performed exploratory surgery and needed to decide whether to remove the bullet, which was lodged in an extremely dangerous and difficult place in his spine. Or they could simply treat the wound and close it up, leaving the slug inside to possibly cause new damage at some future date. Either approach could bring about the detective's premature death.

Mose had immediately phoned "Kia," Sam's wife of eleven years. Within minutes of his call, she canceled all her appointments and rushed to the hospital. Kianah, Hawai'ian for moon goddess, was a robust Hawai'ian with olive skin, full lips, and a mane of chestnut-brown hair that curled about her neck. Black-framed glasses seemed only to enhance her eyes, the color of coffee brewing. Now, in the hospital waiting room, she had to make the most important decision of her life. They had married right after Sam's graduation from the Honolulu Police Academy. She loved her husband deeply and passionately. But his dangerous profession had taken its toll on her. She could never quite suppress the knot of fear that, at times, wore her down. At this moment what she feared most was the prospect of bringing up their nine-year-old daughter, Peggy, alone. She saw Sam's doctor coming down the hall toward her.

"Mrs. Nahoe, he's awake now and wants to see you before he goes back into surgery. He wants us to close up the wound. He says he'll take his chances for now." The decision had been made for her.

* * * *

9

After a month's hospital stay and four months of intense physical therapy, Sam emerged to face the grim truth. He had a troublesome walking gait, a serious limp, and a considerably bent-over back. To overcome it, he needed not one, but two metal canes. He chose a pair in a subtle pattern of maroon and navy blue with curved, foam-cushioned handles. These canes were not just for balance; they granted him the means to stand straight and the ability to walk, even if only for short distances. They carried his full 220-pound weight with each step. The bullet that lurked in his spine remained the culprit—a constant reminder of the unknown, the potential to cripple further.

In a lighter moment, he dubbed his walking canes "Cane" and "Able." No, not Cain and Abel, the biblical spellings—he liked the play on words. Sam soon learned to support his shifted weight by coordinating each leg with the opposite cane, much in the same manner as the motion of a cross-country skier. "Ski-walking," he called it. He could manage decently enough with a single cane, but quickly tired of that mode when he discovered it put his full weight on his right shoulder and would just create a new problem for him: rotator cuff damage.

Sam's birth name was actually Kamuela, Hawai'ian for Samuel. He appreciated his heritage, but as a police officer he felt his name often got in the way, especially for most folks during emergencies on the phone. He preferred to be called Kam, but somehow it never took, so by default, he decided to be Sam, which was what his wife called him anyway.

He would be back on the job soon—or so he thought. His spirits had remained high throughout the recovery period, despite the awkward gait and a constant aching in the lower back. But a week after returning to his squad room, the captain himself handed him an envelope. A forced retirement notice. It came not only with a commendation for solving his last crime, but a commendation for saving the life of a fellow officer. Plus a disability pension and health benefits.

But no matter how generous, the retirement hit Sam hard.

Silently, he protested. *I'm a damned good cop, only thirty-six, with a promising career. And I'm not trained for anything else.* He wasn't even offered a desk job, although he would have hated it. But it would have been better than walking the plank, as he viewed it.

In a matter of days, Sam Nahoe underwent a metamorphosis from an easy-going, loving husband and father to a demanding, sullen grouch. There was no living with him. At home alone all day, with Kia downtown in her successful law practice and Peggy in school, he refined the art of sulking. Following three months of constant morose bitchiness, Kia's pity and even her love grew thin. Threats of divorce mounted. In June, after a major shrieking skirmish, Sam moved out to his own apartment. But the trial separation resolved nothing, with each one blaming the other, and Peggy hopelessly begging them to reconcile. The divorce became final the following February. He reluctantly surrendered child custody in return for weekly Sunday visitations.

Sam spent more than a few evenings a week sopping up suds at Charlie's Bar and Grille over on Wai'alae Avenue. Often he shared a few beers with a fellow police retiree, who got sick of commiserating and tossed out a new idea for him. "Hey, pal, why don't you drive a cab?"

Sam thought it over—for fifteen minutes. *Not a bad idea*, he decided. He could keep busy, earn a little extra cash, and still stay off his feet. Besides, driving might even be therapeutic. Convinced, he took the cash settlement for his disability and bought a used, but well-maintained Checker Cab, bright yellow, with a surrounding black and white checkered stripe just under the windows. He had no trouble obtaining all the necessary licensing to become an independent owner/driver. It wasn't long before Sam had a regular clientele, freelance fares that took him throughout the island of O'ahu. It proved to be a lonely life, but he became a much calmer man now that he had a job—a job where people actually depended on him.

On one of his Sunday afternoons with his daughter, he took Peggy to the Honolulu Zoo. A miniature of her mother, she had a sturdy body and chestnut-brown hair woven into two thick braids. She had also acquired the dawning of cruel wisdom that comes from a child witnessing her parents' divorce.

They strolled past the gazelles and other African animals. "Know what, Daddy?" Peggy said. "You need a pet. Then you wouldn't be so lonely."

Sam looked down at her and grinned. "Are you suggesting I get myself a zebra?"

She giggled. "Of course not, Daddy. How about a dog or a cat?"

"It wouldn't be right to leave an animal alone all day while I drive my cab."

Peggy's eyes danced with an idea, the nine-year-old psychiatrist at work. "Why couldn't the pet sit up front with you?"

"Peggs, that's a crazy idea. But…we'll see. Thanks for worrying about me." He gave her a big squeeze.

The next day Sam dropped off a fare in Moiliili and headed for the Hawai'i Humane Society across the street. *Maybe it's meant to be*, he chuckled to himself.

"Cat or dog?" the attendant asked.

"A dog," Sam promptly replied. He was led down a series of chain-link cages.

Sad canine faces nuzzled against their gates. A few looked promising. Sam stopped cold at one cage, and there he befriended a female eighteen-month-old golden retriever named Goldie.

"Well, mostly golden," assured the vet on duty. "Maybe a slight touch of Doberman."

Guaranteed to eat a lot and shed a lot," Sam thought wryly.

But he fell instantly in love. She had soft, wavy fur that would get glossy when brushed, a plumed tail, and a mouth that curled up at the corners. Goldens were the only breed he knew of that looked like they were always smiling. It was an adoption made in heaven, and took only an hour for the paperwork and loyalty lecture. Within a few weeks he was able to settle Goldie into the passenger seat, her front-row view of Honolulu streets. Of course, she wore her own canine seatbelt harness. Sam had ordered it off the Internet for $39.95.

The ex-policeman and Goldie spent most of their days together in the taxi. Sam ran the air conditioner full time to control the inevitable doggie smell. Two square meals, plus semi-recreational walks, satisfied her daily needs. Goldie proved to be as intelligent as his new owner had hoped, and soon picked up a number of habits.

Whether good or bad remained one's point of view. A few weeks later, when they dropped off the last fare of the day, Sam climbed out of the cab and came around to open the trunk and help the passenger with his luggage. The passenger counted out the exact meter amount, $45, and handed over the bills. Sam held up two fingers behind his back. His new partner poked her head out the window, began a slow growl, and just slightly bared her front teeth. The man blinked in shock and quickly fished another ten-spot out of his wallet. Then Sam held up one finger behind his back. Goldie stopped growling and broke into her usual friendly smile.

"Good girl," he told her afterward, slipping her a Milk Bone.

Yes, Goldie proved useful for his business and also provoked much-needed conversation from the back seat. Many of Sam's patrons were pet lovers. Who couldn't love a smiling golden?

One day, after parking in the PetSmart lot, Sam and Goldie were ski-walking and padding their way toward the store, when they witnessed a purse snatching. The young thief, who looked about seventeen, dodged between cars to escape, and mindlessly ran straight toward them.

Once a cop always a cop. The ex-detective stepped in his way. When the thief tried to shift direction, Sam turned one of his canes into an impromptu weapon. He sharply hooked Able's handle around the thief's ankle, causing him to trip and fall on his face. Sam stooped to pick up the stolen purse, let go of the dog's leash, and said "Go, girl!" Goldie placed both front paws and much of her sixty-five-pound weight on the teenage boy's back. As he struggled to get free, Sam held up two fingers for Goldie. She growled and bared her teeth next to the thief's face. To her it was a game.

It's a good thing this loser doesn't know goldens are charmers, not fighters, thought Sam, as he approached the two.

A quick frisking let Sam know the teenager wasn't armed. Adding his own left foot to Goldie's paws in the middle of the perp's back, he cell-phoned HPD headquarters for assistance. The victim rushed over to retrieve her purse and offered him a reward. But Sam, still thinking like the honest cop he'd always been, refused. Instead, he gave her his business card: "Copper and Goldie Taxi Service," complete with phone number and email address—and Goldie's picture on the reverse side.

Sam had no way of predicting that this "collar" was the beginning of their crime-fighting adventures.

§

A Dead Man Isn't Fare

THE MAJOR CAB COMPANIES CONSIDERED SAM NAHOE ONE step above a gypsy, an unlicensed, illegal taxi. Although he was licensed and independent, they thought of him as an aggressive nuisance—a fare stealer. So what? Didn't bother him a bit.

Sam reached out and stroked his lady friend's bronze-colored head as she sat in her spiffy seatbelt harness. His unlikely companion rode beside him as he drove fares all over the city and county of Honolulu. He loved the city streets in spite of the congestion rife with three rush hours—yes, three: morning, noon, and evening. More than a million cars crisscrossed the island of O'ahu daily and they all seemed to be going where he needed to be.

Today, as Sam cruised the downtown and waited for a green traffic light, Goldie let out a sharp bark. A young blond-haired man was pounding on the passenger window next to her.

"Are you available?" he shouted and stepped back up on the curb.

Sam nodded and eased the cab into a nearby parking space. The man climbed into the back seat and shut the door. Sam looked over his shoulder.

15

"Where to, brah?"

At first the fare remained silent. Then, in his rumpled shirt and half-closed lids, he took a deep, heaving breath and, barely above a whisper, gave an address in a remote area of Kailua. Still, Sam smiled. A sixty-dollar ride to the windward shore, and he even knew the street. But he felt uncomfortable—something about the man's demeanor. He eyed his passenger in the rear-view mirror. What he saw did not look good. *Is he in pain with his face all scrunched up like a prune?* Sam took another peek after emerging from the tunnels at the crest of the Pali, a highway through the Koʻolau mountain cliffs. The young man's head was drooped, propped in the corner by the window. *Asleep*, Sam figured. Goldie decided to take her nap as well, so he tuned the radio to the University of Hawaiʻi 'Bows baseball game. Twenty-five minutes later, he pulled up to the Kailua address, a mustard-colored two-story house with a grossly neglected lawn.

"Okay, brah, this is the address you gave me." Sam read the charge on the meter to him, but the man didn't move. Didn't even pick up his head. The cabbie repeated the numbers on the meter. Still no response. *Something's not right,* he decided, *and even Goldie senses it.* He unclipped her harness, pulled himself out of the car, and walked around to the lawn. Letting Goldie out first, he opened the fare's door. His passenger began to fall toward him. Sam quickly caught him, propped him upright, and gently re-settled him into the back seat.

There's no blood or outward signs of violence, Sam noted. He checked the man's pulse. It had gone south the way his cab fare was about to go. *The poor guy.* Death must smell something awful and threatening to a dog because Goldie whined and backed away from the cab. Sam checked the man's pockets. No wallet, no money, no ID. *I've been had!*

Goldie started barking, facing the house, her head raised. Sam looked up in time to see someone ducking behind a curtain on the second floor. "Good dog. Someone here must know him."

What had once been a doorbell now hung by a wire. Sam

knuckle-knocked several times. No response. With closed fist, he pounded on the wooden door of this shingle-covered, dilapidated dwelling set among ironwood trees. The next house stood half a block away. There was no name on the door or on the mailbox at the street. After hooking Goldie to her leash, they trudged around back and found a Ford Taurus caked with dirt, parked on the gravel driveway. Sam figured it to be pretty old, maybe a 2001 model. He could tell the original color was white, but doubted it had been washed since then. It had Maui license plates; he recorded the plate numbers on the back of his fare log. The vehicle was locked, but a lady's nylon stocking had caught underneath the front passenger door. Goldie saw it first and gave it a complete sniff-over.

Back at the cab, Sam tried calling the police on his cell. Not one teensy bar showed. His charger plug had fallen out of its socket and lay useless on the floor. Without a company dispatcher, that phone existed purely to pump the life blood into his taxi business. He plugged it back in and wondered how many calls he'd missed. Next came the hard part: dealing with his unfortunate passenger. Sam carefully opened the back door and strapped the body into its proper seatbelt. With Goldie and the dead man secured into their seats, Sam set out back over the Pali Highway to the city and Honolulu Police Department headquarters at 801 North Beretania Street. He drove into the underground precinct lot and entered the rear door of the building, leaving Goldie to reluctantly guard the corpse.

Sam asked for Corporal Mose Kauahi, his former partner and friend, whom he dropped in on now and then. After a short wait on a hard wooden bench, Mose appeared, looking the same with his rust-brown uncombed hair and an outdoorsy complexion.

"Hey Sam, how the hell are you?" he asked, extending a hand.

Sam shook it. "Fine."

"You don't look so fine. In fact, you look kinda frazzled around the edges."

17

Sam forced a miserable little smile. "I've got a special delivery out back for you. Come see for yourself." Mose followed him out to the cab. Sam gave him a detailed account, including a description of the sad Kailua house, the Taurus's license plate number, and most important, someone peeking out from behind a curtain in a second-floor window.

"You touch anything, Sam?"

"I know the drill, man. But, yeah, I propped him up and put him in the seatbelt. Had to. That's all."

"And he seemed okay when he hailed you? No marks or noises?"

"Nothing noticeable. At first he seemed okay. He gave me that address, didn't he? But he didn't say anything else. Maybe a grunt or two before he went to sleep. At least, I thought he was asleep."

"You're gonna hafta leave your cab with us—until the crime scene people and Medical Examiner (ME) get through with it. We'll get you and the dog a ride home."

"Mind if I stick around and tag along with you? I'm not exactly John Q. Public, you know."

Mose looked uncomfortable, shifting his eyes to the ground. "Technically, Sam, you're a suspect. But if it's okay with Danny we'll go out on a limb for you and keep you in the loop."

A spasm gripped Sam's chest. He was a suspect? But he chose to keep cool and asked, "Danny?"

"Yah! Danny Oshiro, my new partner. We'll need to drive over to that Kailua house now."

Inside the station once more, Mose introduced Sam to his partner, and they brought the sergeant up to date. Danny put in calls to the ME and the mobile crime scene unit, while Mose arranged a car for the drive to the Kailua house.

Meanwhile, Goldie and Sam were relegated to the same wooden bench to await further developments. The dog sat patiently next to him, behaving herself. But the whole scene felt unpleasant to Sam. A sour taste filled his mouth. Of course Mose had a new partner. Why hadn't it even occurred to him? In denial, that's why. And this friggin' bench was for victims. For perps. Not for the likes of him. He missed being a cop.

In the next hour, Mose reported back with surprising news. The Ford Taurus was gone and the unfurnished house was deserted. The back door lock had been jimmied, and there were signs of someone hiding out there—maybe a man and a woman. He and Danny had found two air mattresses on a bedroom floor. In the fridge, a couple of beers, but no food. They found a small tube of toothpaste, mostly used up, on the bathroom sink.

Mose had been able to reach the owner of record, who was shocked to learn that his rental property had been broken into and lived in. He was planning on renovating before renting it out again. Mose put out a BOLO (Be On the Lookout) for the missing vehicle.

After the crime scene investigators finished with Sam's cab, the ME's people carted the body off. The crime scene crew declared his vehicle's back seat "clean and not the scene of any violent activity." At last, cabbie, cab, and dog were free to go.

By now it was 7 p.m. At least one of them was starving and the other would gladly eat anything anytime. Sam drove to a tiny Korean takeout place on the corner of Kinau and Keʻeaumoku and pulled into one of the few diagonal spots out front. The large sign above the door read "Itchy Butt – Chicken & Joy." The logo, between "Itchy" and "Butt," portrayed a bare-chested cartoon chicken with attitude: dark glasses, a Mohawk haircut, and patterned shorts—dancing on its two skinny legs. Sam's kind of place. As he unclipped Goldie's harness, the golden squeezed herself into the driver's seat and sat up straight with both front paws on the steering wheel—waiting for Sam to crown her with his cabbie's peaked cap. That done, her owner leaned over for a reassuring tongue slurp.

Through the take-out window, Sam ordered the bowl of Korean fried chicken and rice with spiced mayo for himself and a *loco moco*: a hamburger topped with a fried egg on a bed of rice, smothered in brown gravy. He intended to give Goldie half and save the rest for his own supper. He prepaid and stood to one side to wait for his order. He had noticed the one man waiting at the window, but now there was a woman in line behind him. Suddenly, Sam heard barking. He'd know that bark anywhere. He hobbled on his canes the few feet to the parking lot and stared. His cab was empty! Goldie had jumped through the open driver's window and was sniffing and scratching at the car parked on the far side next to his. A muddy Ford Taurus. Sam checked the license plate. He could hardly believe his luck: the same Ford that was in the backyard at the Kailua house. Goldie tugged at the errant nylon stocking still hanging out the bottom of the front passenger door.

Glancing back at the Itchy Butt, Sam noticed that the lone woman customer was still at the take-out window, either still pondering her order or waiting for it. Safely out of her direct line of view, he ski-walked to the Ford. The driver's-side window was rolled down. Reaching in, he released the hood latch and moved to the front of the car. Leaning Cane and Able on a front fender, he lifted the hood, deftly unhooked the distributor cap, and eased the hood back down until it latched once more.

Goldie was still toying with the nylon stocking. "Good girl, that's enough now," Sam said. Grabbing her by the collar, he opened his cab door, and gave her a push on the ʻōkole to guide her up into the front seat.

His cell phone was full of all kinds of bars now, and he managed to reach his former partner at his desk. Sam gave him all the information, and Mose alerted a patrol car in the vicinity. He and Danny Oshiro were on their way as well.

Sam figured his order should be ready, so he stepped back to the take-out window. Sure enough, it sat on the counter in two white paper bags with the usual tantalizing grease spots. Back in the cab, he started gobbling up chicken and rice out of the Styrofoam container. Goldie inhaled the entire *loco moco* from her plastic bowl that was screwed permanently to the floorboard in the front passenger side. *Damn!* He'd intended to only give her half. *I'd better pay more attention,* he thought, *or she'll get too fat to be my helper.*

Partway through his own lunch, the woman left the window with her order, and he took full notice of her for the first time. Jet-black hair cut straight across, ending just below her ears. Pleasant face, no makeup. A gray clinging dress revealed her slight frame. Dimpled cheeks, the left side more pronounced than the right. She climbed into the Taurus. *This must be the woman who had peeked out from behind the curtain at the house. A link to my dead passenger!*

Moments later, he heard her engine starter grinding away. The woman didn't give up easily. Soon desperation worked its way into the starter's voice. She tried again—a dying whine, then nothing. Her car door squeaked open as she emerged. Afraid she'd walk away before the police arrived, Sam set his rice bowl on the dashboard, wiped his chin and lips with the thin paper napkin, and got out of the cab. Approaching the Taurus, he hoped she wouldn't recognize him. Goldie, refusing to be left behind, squeezed her furry bulk after him.

"Ma'am? Sounds like you're having car trouble. Mind if I have a look under the hood?"

The woman hesitated before answering. "It won't start. I don't know what to do," she said, swallowing hard.

Sam sensed that her fright went way beyond car trouble. She looked down at his newly arrived sidekick. Goldie licked her hand in a comforting way and sat down beside her.

"Okay. Please see what you can do," she replied in a quavering voice.

"How about you get back in the car and eat your carryout," he told her. He disappeared under the hood and tinkered around noisily. Several minutes later he asked her to try again, knowing full well that it wouldn't start. *Whirrr whirr whirr*—then nothing.

Sam heard a car pull up. Poking his head out, he saw a blue and white police car blocking the Taurus's retreat. He quickly restored the distributor cap, flipped the two clips on to secure it, and dropped the hood back into place.

The officer had already reached the driver's side window. He requested the woman to produce the car's registration and her driver's license. While he perused the documents, a second vehicle pulled up next to the first. Mose and Danny got out and walked over to the Taurus.

"I'll take over from here," said Mose, flashing his badge. The officer nodded and handed over the two documents. Mose glanced at the name and Nevada address. "Cindy Prell from Las Vegas?"

"Yes."

"You are a person of interest in a murder investigation," declared Mose in his most officious voice.

"Mmmurder?" Cindy stammered. "Who was murdered?"

"I'll ask the questions here," replied Mose.

His deflective response informed Sam that the police had not yet gotten an ID back from the victim's prints. Sam ski-walked over to his cab, leaned casually against the front fender, and took in the exchange. *Okay, they call it eavesdropping,* he reminded himself. *But I have the right. They wouldn't be here without me.*

"We know your vehicle was parked at a Kailua address at 1 p.m. today," said Danny. "Miss Prell, were you at that address then?"

"Yes, sir," she whispered. Her hand flew up to cover her neck and chest. She wished she wasn't wearing such a revealing neckline.

"Did you see a cab stop out front and the driver knock at the front door?"

"I…I…Maybe."

"Either you did or did not, ma'am," scolded the sergeant. "The driver saw you at the upstairs window. I can have him identify you if you like."

I doubt that, Sam thought.

"Yes, I saw him," Cindy whimpered.

"Then why didn't you answer the door?" asked Danny.

"We were afraid."

"We? I thought you were alone."

"I was alone. Will hadn't returned yet. At first I thought that was him in the cab. I couldn't answer the door to just anyone that showed up."

"Does this Will have a last name?"

"Of course, Will Barington. He's my fiancé."

"What were you doing in an abandoned house?"

"We were both in hiding."

"Hiding from what or who? Who are you afraid of, Miss Prell?"

"Thor Morgan, the security chief at Trippe Industries," said Cindy. "They followed us here to Hawai'i."

"They?" inquired Danny. "This Morgan fellow and who else?"

"His boss, Leland Jameson, the CEO. The chief executive officer," Cindy added, her voice stronger now.

"Just why would these people be following you and threatening you as well?"

"Will used to be a bookkeeper at Trippe—that is, until he decided to become a whistleblower."

"Whistleblower!" Danny repeated. "What's that all about?"

"A while back, Will was going over the books, doing his routine monthly internal audit. He discovered that Mr. Jameson had transferred a large chunk of money, $200,000, from the employees' pension fund to his own personal compensation account, using some phony expenditures as a cover-up. When Will confronted him, Mr. Jameson claimed he had invested the money in a sure thing and would return it in ninety days. He said it would accrue interest and beef up the employees' fund. 'End of discussion,' he told Will."

Cindy felt braver now, crossed her arms firmly over her chest, and continued. "But Will was really angry. He knew that the only sure investment is Treasuries, but the yield these days on a three-month Treasury is pathetic: less than 2 percent. He did some digging on his own and discovered that Mr. Jameson had put a large down-payment on a million-dollar condo apartment in San Francisco. And guess how much he put down: $200,000! Will confronted him and threatened to go to the police unless the entire amount was returned immediately to the employees' pension fund. He was told to back off—or else."

Cindy stopped to take a breath. Sam was following her responses closely. He saw that she had changed before his very eyes from a timid little gal to a confident young woman who obviously knew something about finance.

Mose was also listening intently and asked her the next obvious question: "Ms. Prell, you seem to know a lot about all this. Do you have a job?"

"Oh, yes. I'm the office manager of a boutique in Las Vegas. I took a short leave of absence to accompany Will here. He told me everything. He insisted on going to the police anyway. That's when Mr. Jameson called in Thor Morgan, his security chief, to rough him up, or at least threaten to. Thor brought out a blackjack from his pocket and dangled it back and forth in front of Will's face. Will said that was plenty scary. Thor told him to return to his job and keep his mouth shut."

Mose stepped closer. "Ma'am? How'd you happen to wind up here in Honolulu, anyway?"

Cindy's cheeks flushed, determined to do right by her lover. "I convinced Will we needed to get out of Vegas in a hurry, but out of town wasn't enough. Mr. Jamison sent Thor after us. The big thug with his cauliflower ear almost caught up with us in San Diego, so we took the next plane here. We bought this junker car and were planning to move here. Things looked good for about a month. I've been job-hunting. But yesterday I just happened to see Mr. Jameson going into the Great Adventures Hotel on Ala Moana Boulevard with Thor right behind. When I told Will I saw them, he decided he had to meet with Mr. Jameson and convince him that he had no intention of going to the police anymore. They had nothing to fear from him; he just wanted to be free of the whole mess. So Will set up a meeting with his boss at the Great Adventures for this peace-making parley. That was supposed to take place in room 209 at ten this morning. I haven't heard from Will since I left around nine to go out to Starbucks."

"Ms. Prell," Mose said, "I'd like you to come down to police headquarters with me. There are more questions that need to be answered, and I'd like you to make an identification for me."

"Identification? You mean the dead man is my Will?"

"Not necessarily, ma'am," said Danny, "but we need to be sure. We'll bring you back to your car afterward." He held the cruiser door open for her.

"Mind if I tag along in my cab?" Sam asked.

"Suit yourself, Sam."

"Why him?" asked Cindy. "He was just helping me start my car."

"Ma'am, he's the taxi driver you snubbed this afternoon. We found the deceased in the back seat of his cab."

"Oh, no!" Cindy's expression froze with the impact of this information as she slowly sank into the cruiser's back seat.

Sam caught a few traffic lights and made a short stop for Goldie to attend to nature, so they arrived at headquarters somewhat behind Mose, Danny, and Cindy. They'd already taken her down to the morgue to identify the body. While he waited, Sam made a call to the Great Adventures Hotel and asked the desk clerk if Mr. Leland Jameson had checked out of room 209 yet.

"No sir, I believe he's staying one more day. We just sent up room service. Would you like me to put you through to the room?"

"No, thanks. I'll drop by to see him in the morning." Sam shook his head and smiled wryly at the indiscretion of the desk clerk. *No guest privacy in that hotel.*

Just then, he saw Mose and Cindy coming down the hall toward him. The tears streamed down her face, leading him to believe she had identified her fiancé's body. Mose informed him of the early autopsy results.

"He was severely beaten about the midsection and died

slowly—internal bleeding most likely from the extreme trauma."

Slowly enough to reach the cab and give me the Kailua address, Sam thought.

"Apparently, the beater wore three rings on his punching hand." Mose displayed two enlarged photographs where the rings had left distinctive markings on Will's abdomen.

Sam told Mose about the call to the Great Adventures. He and Danny quickly put together a team of two officers in Kevlar vests and headed toward the bridge side of Waikīkī. Not wanting to miss any of the action, Goldie and Sam followed close behind. At the hotel Sam left Goldie in the driver's seat wearing his peaked cabbie cap and followed the team. Room 209 was at the end of the corridor, adjacent to the door leading to the stairwell. Danny instructed Sam and the team to keep in the shadows while Mose knocked. The door opened halfway.

"Mr. Leland Jameson?"

"Who wants to know?"

"Detectives Kauahi and Oshiro, HPD." They flashed their badges. "We'd like to ask you a few questions. Okay if we come in?" Without waiting for an answer, they pushed their way inside, leaving the door slightly ajar.

"What's the beef, Detectives? I'm a busy man."

Mose asked, "Are you familiar with a William Barington from Las Vegas, Nevada?"

"He used to be a bookkeeper in my firm."

"Used to be?"

"Yes," said Jameson smoothly. "He up and quit a month ago without giving any reason. I thought it was a little strange. I had to get a replacement immediately. Have to keep Payroll and Purchasing up and running, you know."

Peeking in, Sam was able to see and hear everything. Jameson, although short in stature, looked like a successful businessman in a well-tailored suit, white shirt, and tie.

Danny stared down at the man, unblinking. "Mr. Jameson, we understand that you had a meeting scheduled in this room with

26

Mr. Barington for ten o'clock this morning. Did the meeting take place?"

"Here in Honolulu? Of course not. I assume Will is in Las Vegas looking for another job. Say, what's this all about? I don't like your attitude, Detective."

"That's a shame, Mr. Jameson. You know what happens when you lose your memory while speaking to the police, don't you? By the way, sir, do you know a Mr. Thor Morgan?"

"Of course. He's a security officer for my company. What of it?"

"Did this Mr. Morgan travel here with you to Honolulu?"

"Yes, but why shouldn't he? Corporation executives aren't always safe traveling alone. Say, what the hell's going on? What's your beef with me?"

"Tell me, sir, was it your intent to use Morgan's muscle here in Honolulu?"

Jameson tried to puff up his narrow chest, and said, "Detective, that's one helluva crude question. Of course not. I don't know anything about any rough stuff. Now, I would like to see my lawyer before answering any more of your outrageous questions."

"Fine," said Danny. "We'll continue down at the station where we can wait for your lawyer to arrive. Meanwhile, you can relax in one of our deluxe cells there. We'll be holding you as a material witness."

Just then, Sam heard heavy footsteps clomping up the stairs from the floor below. He edged himself out the stairwell door. A reckless thing to do, he knew, but in his khaki shorts and aloha shirt, on two canes, Sam figured he wouldn't look like much of a threat to anyone.

A huge, ugly galoot in a T-shirt and sweatpants trudged up the stairs. It had to be Thor Morgan. Sam stumbled out of the way as the guy, stinking of sweat and tobacco breath, barreled past him. But not before Sam saw both the man's hands. They were covered with heavily jeweled gold rings. Breathing hard from exertion, the thug reached for the door and saw the police team waiting in the hall.

He jerked his bulk around, bumping and slamming Sam out of his way, and missing steps as he lurched back down the stairs. Two of the waiting officers took off after him. Pumped full of adrenaline, Sam re-entered the corridor, ski-walked to the elevator, and took it to the lobby. Using Cane and Able with greater speed than even he knew was possible, he came out of the double glass doors just in time to see the thug emerge onto the street and charge toward his Checker Cab with its open windows.

Thor pulled open the rear door and climbed in. "The airport, and step on it, Mac!" he shouted.

Sam halted just a few feet away. Trying hard not to laugh, he watched his trusted partner at work. Goldie, still wearing his peaked cap, squeezed her large body around, placed her front paws on the seat back, and loomed in the thug's face—growling like a pro, even without Sam's two-finger prompting.

"What the hell?" Thor boomed. "A damned mutt? Where's the friggin' driver?"

He tried to backhand the dog's head out of his way, but succeeded only in knocking the precious cap off. That meant war to Goldie. She chomped down hard on his hairy arm just above the wrist, pulling it down toward the front seat so that Thor couldn't get any leverage with his free arm. This tactic lasted long enough for the pursuing officers to take charge, haul the escaping thug out of the vehicle, and cuff him. One officer read him his rights and led him away in the patrol car. Goldie sat in the driver's seat grinning and thumping her tail up and down. Sam pulled out the bag of Milk Bones from the glove compartment. It took three before she'd surrender the driver's seat to him. He gave her a grand hug afterward. He couldn't be prouder of Goldie's bravery.

Sam had almost forgotten about Cindy Prell until he saw her slumped and fast asleep on the bench back at the precinct. Tapping her gently on the shoulder, he woke her and offered to drive her back to her car.

"Yes, please. Thank God they've been arrested." Her sea-green eyes shone with tearful gratitude. "I thought we were going to spend the rest of our lives running from them. "Oh, it's so unfair. Will and I had planned such a lovely life together."

All the way to the Itchy Butt she leaned forward to tickle Goldie behind the ears. Sam pulled the cab into an empty space, climbed out, and followed Cindy to the Taurus. Before she could even open the door he confessed his part in her ignition problem. She wanted to get angry, but couldn't. Starting her engine on the first try, she let it idle. Sam had jumper cables in case it didn't. "Thank you for everything, Sam. You've been wonderful." She flashed him a dimpled smile, and for the first time he saw a slight gap between her two front teeth. *Rather fetching*, he decided.

"Aw, shucks, ma'am," he drawled comically, sliding his thumbs into his pockets like an Old West cowboy.

"Do you have a place to stay tonight?" he asked.

"I'll bunk down at the Kailua house and start looking for temp work in the morning. I don't really feel like going back to Vegas just now. Too many painful memories."

"I'll tell you what, Cindy. Follow me over to my Auntie Momi's house. She's got a spare bedroom right now, and you can stay there till you get back on your feet."

She poked her head out the driver's side window. "Are you sure it'll be all right with her?"

"Oh, yeah. Auntie's always complaining that she's lonely, and I don't visit her enough. It'll be a perfect match. Besides, it'll be a good excuse for Goldie and me to visit her more often." Sam leaned over and planted a brief, friendly peck on Cindy's still-damp cheek.

The next thing he knew, she had slung her right arm around his neck in a full squeeze. Grateful, or something more, he couldn't say.

* * * *

The Assistant District Attorney (ADA) filed a series of charges, ranging from aggravated assault to murder in the second degree. Thor's rings proved to be a perfect match for the purple punch markings on Will Barington's abdomen. The thug, who was known among his cohorts simply as Thor, implicated his boss, Leland Jameson, in return for the lesser charges. But still he protested. "Hey, I just roughed Will up a little. Just enough so he wouldn't squeal on my boss about the 200K. I didn't hurt him that bad."

"Oh no?" the ADA challenged. "Then why is that poor, defenseless man dead from your beating? Dead because he tried to protect the employees' pension fund."

During the ADA's investigation, he learned a little something about this man he was prosecuting. Thor's real first name was Eugene. He admitted that the name "Thor" came from his teenage fighting days, when he was always "sore." Apparently, a speech impediment, a lisp he could never get rid of, turned it into "Thor." To overcome the humiliation, he became a corporate muscle man.

Episode Three

Death by the Pixel

S AM SAT ON A PARK BENCH READING THE HOMETOWN PAPER. Peggy, just turned eleven, sat next to him, tinkering with her brand-new digital camera, Sam's birthday gift to her. Goldie lay asleep, curled up at their feet.

Peggy slid the flash card back into the camera and turned to Sam. "Daddy, do you still miss being a policeman?"

"Sometimes, sweetheart, but then I never would have met Goldie, would I?"

"You're right about that, Daddy. But why did you want to become a policeman in the first place?"

Sam laid his paper down, stretched his arms over the back of the bench, and crossed his legs. "There was this very old man, a *kupuna* named Kona Nala, who lived next door to Auntie Momi. He was a retired sergeant from HPD and loved to *talk story* from the old days. Every story was a big adventure. When I look back, I think he may have made some of them up. I'll never know for sure. Auntie Momi didn't get along with him, so your Auntie Eva and I used to sneak over and sit on his lanai glider at the back of the house and listen. He kept his refrigerator out on that lanai, so he'd always pour us some POG before he started. Anyway, his stories inspired me to become a policeman." Sam made a mental note to buy the sweet, thick pineapple-orange-guava drink for his own fridge.

"Gee, Daddy, I wish I had my own personal *kupuna* like that." She bounced to her feet. "Time for picture-taking." She skipped off a few yards, and began snapping shots of every bird and bloom in sight. Sam's gaze followed her, sharing her excitement as she zoomed in on a *kōlea*, a Pacific golden plover newly arrived from the Arctic for the winter; a clutch of spotted doves with their blue-encircled eyes and polka-dotted necks; and the pink blossoms of a tecoma tree. Then he returned to the sports pages for the details on the Padres' latest win, only occasionally glancing up to check on his daughter. In a rare moment of inattention, he didn't see her move out of sight. When her first high-pitched shrieks erupted, Goldie's ears flew north.

The shrieks came from behind a flowering hedge, where Peggy was taking pictures of fuchsia bougainvillea. Her anguished voice set her father's muscled hulk in motion. Clumsily grabbing Goldie's leash, he heaved up onto his canes. Huffing heavily from moving the two canes in alternating rapid succession, he rounded the corner of the tall hedge and discovered his daughter lying prone in the grass, her arms and legs flailing. The first cries had now shrunk to gasping sobs. Goldie lurched forward, jerked the leash out of his hand, and loped to Peggy's side.

The distraught and clueless father knelt as quickly as he could and flipped his only child face-up. "What's wrong, sweetheart! What happened?" No answer. More sobs. Sam gently brushed away the braids flopping across her damp face, then searched carefully, but saw no apparent injury or impending threat to his precious youngster in her striped T-shirt and jeans.

Peggy, too upset to respond, kept stabbing through the air with her forefinger toward a dark object lying ten feet away in the grass. The new digital camera.

"What about the camera?" Sam asked as he held and rocked her in his arms. "What's wrong with it, sweetheart?"

Peggy's lips formed the letter P, and with additional effort, the words "Horrible picture" exploded. Sam helped Peggy to her feet, and arm-in-arm, the two approached the hastily abandoned camera. He scooped it up and brushed off several grass blades. Pressing the "DISPLAY" control, he refreshed the last picture taken. Out of the corner of his eye he saw Peggy shudder as the image materialized. Then she knelt down, buried her face in Goldie's neck, and got rewarded with slobbering licks.

Sam froze as he stared at the last image. The photograph was of a hideous crime scene, apparently in a bedroom: a bloody multiple stabbing of a young adult female in a white dress. She lay stretched out on the bed, her head up against the brass headboard, in a strangely placid pose. Sam didn't recognize the ashen-faced brunette.

"What the devil is this?" he muttered. The camera was new. He'd bought it online at a good price. Had the terrorizing picture been embedded before he even received it? He forwarded ahead, then backspaced through earlier images to see if there were more crime scene shots. None. Instead, the bewildered father found pictures of monkeypod trees and the cascading bougainvillea—shots his daughter had taken a few minutes earlier here in Kaka'ako Waterfront Park. They were for her sixth-grade science project due on Wednesday.

Sam found no other photos residing on the memory card. Backing up from the crime scene photo, he noted that all of Peggy's shots were in sequence—one through eight, with number nine being the horrific invasive one. Exploring the camera's programmable controls, he discovered that the date/time feature had been turned off. Alarm bells went off in his head. *Hey! What's going on?* He had set the date and time himself before gift-wrapping the camera.

Oh, great, he thought. *Just what I need. A gruesome glitch on one of our precious days together. This could throw a serious monkey wrench into the divorce agreement.* He and Kia had worked it out to make the split as painless as possible for their little daughter. Kia had demanded neither alimony nor child support, instead allowing Sam and Peggy to hang out together every Sunday at one of

Honolulu's beach parks. It was the best deal he could negotiate in the court-ordered agreement. Sundays had always been treasured happy hours for them. Now they might all be in jeopardy.

"Daddy, this is your fault. You're responsible. You gave me this creepy camera. How could you?" she wailed. "I want my mommy!"

Unable to reason with his hysterical daughter, Sam took her home. As usual, his ex-wife sided with Peggy.

Sam pleaded his case. "I'm telling you, Kia, I have no idea how that picture got on the freakin' camera. I bought it brand-new. I promise you I'll get to the bottom of this."

She stared at him with accusing dark eyes. Her attorney's logic evaporated when protecting her child. Refusing to even listen, she stood to her full robust height, and nearly shoved him out the door.

Deflated and not a little disappointed, he decided to go to his former HPD unit with the camera and crime scene shot. There were questions to be answered—a lot of them. *Maybe my old buddies can help me.* But before heading to HPD headquarters, he dropped Goldie off at his place, leaving her with a bowl of Kibble and fresh water.

He found Danny Oshiro, one of four detectives still in the Homicide unit office on Sunday duty, and showed him the ghastly shot of a crime scene. Danny's wiry frame sprang to attention. "What the hell, Sam! Where did you get this? We don't have a record of any such crime. Not recently, anyway. How old is this picture?"

"I don't know, Danny. My daughter discovered it this afternoon in the camera I bought her online."

Detective Oshiro needed a hard copy of the crime photo to pass around, so he dumped the memory card images into his work computer and copied Peggy's photos of flowers, birds, and trees onto a brand-new memory card. After a little insider persuasion, Danny also provided Sam with a hard copy of the crime picture. He finished a cover message, and emailed it and the photo to all

Homicide and Missing Persons units on the island of O'ahu. As an afterthought, he included a few units on the neighbor islands. Sam knew there wasn't much more this frustrated detective could do. Danny didn't have a body or even a crime scene to investigate. Just a bloody picture.

Sam replaced the memory card in the birthday camera with the new one, thinking, *I'll return the camera to Peggy tomorrow morning. Maybe the two gals in my life will have cooled down by then.* Although he doubted it, and wouldn't blame them if they didn't. Parking the camera and photograph on top of the filing cabinet, he ambled over to the vending machine and slid a dollar in the slot. Munching on a Milky Way, he lingered there to schmooze with a dispatcher on her break.

He returned to the filing cabinet to personally annotate the crime photo with his initial observations and impressions. To his amazement and distress, some of the photo data had already been entered. Despite the fact that the camera's time/date stamping had originally been turned off, the time, 11:23 p.m., and the date, 10.08.13, stared back at him. *Today is Sunday, the sixth. The eighth isn't coming 'til Tuesday. How could that be? A camera malfunction? Someone playing with my head?*

Sam looked around. Everyone had left. He could have sworn there were at least three other people in the room when he'd gone out into the hall. When he entered the men's room he did see Mose Kauahi there and got a friendly "Aloha" from him, but now there was no one else around.

Mose and Sam had been partners in the CID for years. They'd often gone to ballgames and a favorite bar together and had even taken the detective sergeant's exam on the same day. They both passed, only Mose didn't score quite high enough to get promoted. Sam had felt uneasy about his friend being left behind, but knew Mose wouldn't hold a grudge. He was too good a cop and still a grateful friend. In fact, the slug Sam took would have taken Mose down instead.

Sam tore a page from the lined pad on Danny's desk and

wrote a note to Peggy proclaiming his own innocence. Placing the camera and note in a used brown paper lunch bag he found next to the coffee machine, he curled the top into a handle, wrapped it around his left cane handle, and headed out the door for home.

As he entered his three-room apartment, a feeling of intense emptiness swept over him. This would normally be the time when he and Peggy would be sitting at his Formica kitchen table eating their take-out Chinese. Peggy liked to show off how well she used chopsticks, much more skillfully than he could. She loved picking up a single grain of rice just to tease him.

Since his forced disability retirement, he'd come to a stark realization. Somehow he managed to get entangled in crime scenes. The crime world had been his life and, ironically, continued to be, even as a cabbie. Like the other veteran cops, on the job he'd been able to take the gut-wrenching sickness awaiting them most days and steel themselves emotionally from it. But things were different now. He was first and foremost a civilian. And a father. His brain was going ballistic over the audacity of this murderer to invade his daughter's privacy. Worst of all, his own family thought him capable of such an evil prank. He still considered Kia family, despite the divorce.

After a hopeless night of fractured nightmares, he awoke at 5 a.m. Monday. A shave and hot shower prepared him for the new day. A fresh polo shirt and khakis finished the job. Almost, that is. His partner needed her Kibble and constitutional. Half an hour later, on their way out the door, Sam carefully picked up the paper bag containing the camera. Its new memory card was safely installed. He snapped Goldie into her harness and drove the fifteen minutes to Kia's apartment house. He slowly climbed the stairs to the third floor with his canes and the camera bag in his left hand and his right hand on the banister. All that and he still he beat the ancient elevator. Quietly, he placed the bag on the floor just outside Kia's door. It was only 6:30 a.m. He decided he might frighten her if he knocked so early.

* * * *

36

Arriving at the office on Monday, Detective Danny Oshiro found a pile of negative replies to his photo inquiries. He and Mose, his inherited partner, had already gone through them and the stack of missing persons bulletins when Sam called in. No one knew or had heard of any victim or crime scene that fit the camera image, so the two detectives returned to their caseload.

Sam and Goldie put a few hundred miles on their cab, whisking fares about Oʻahu over the next two days. When he dropped off his last passenger, she asked for help with her luggage. Sam complied, but only received the meter amount—even after an hour's drive to the North Shore. No tip. And not the first time he'd faced this. *What's wrong with these folks, anyhow?* Sam quickly decided that the first trick he'd taught Goldie had worked before. Why not again? Good practice for his partner. He placed two fingers behind his back, Goldie's cue to stick her large head out the passenger window and growl. The startled lady quickly dug back into her purse and forked over a 20 percent tip. Sam placed one finger behind his back. Goldie stopped growling. He had trained his rescue dog well.

He ended his workday at 11:30 Tuesday night and popped into the Like-Like Drive-In on the corner of Keʻeaumoku and Kanunu Street. He sorely needed Hawaiʻian comfort food right now, and what could be better than a *loco moco*? As he leisurely munched, his cell phone began vibrating in his pocket. It was Danny.

"Sam, you're not going to believe this. At precisely 11:23 tonight, I got an anonymous phone tip. A muffled male voice gave me a detailed address to a crime scene in Waikīkī. We're here now. It looks like the exact crime scene depicted in your bloody photo. Same brunette, same pose, same white dress, and same bloody stains."

"The body must be pretty ripe after so many days," said Sam.

"Naw! Rigor mortis hasn't even started. She's still warm. The assistant ME guesses the murder took place about two hours ago, but the medical lab might narrow that down some. The body

37

is arranged on a bed, with the head against the headboard. The entire crime scene looks staged just like in your photo."

"That sounds impossible," Sam said. "Mind if I join you? I need to see this for myself." He paid and left with the rest of his supper in a take-out box. In ten minutes he reached the address that Danny had given him. Sam left the windows at half-mast and disconnected Goldie's harness so she could roam the front seats. She chose the warm spot on the driver's side and placed her front paws up on the steering wheel like a little kid.

By the time he entered the apartment, three crime scene technicians had already pored over the place. The apartment had been sanitized. No prints, no fibers, nothing. Most of the blood was confined to the victim and her clothes. Nothing on the floor or the bed except for the thoroughly stained pillowcase behind the victim's head. One corner of the dresser smelled of bleach and tested positive for a mere trace of blood, possibly type O, but much too faint for any effective DNA analysis.

Totally mystified and discouraged, Sam returned home at 2 a.m. and found a phone message from Kia instructing him to call her at her office the next day.

Before leaving for work he rang her back, and instantly regretted it. She laced into him so mercilessly that it took five minutes for him to find out why. On Tuesday afternoon she and Peggy had taken more pictures of flowers at Kaka'ako Park with the birthday camera. They'd hurriedly left the park without reviewing the new shots because it started to rain. At home Peggy loaded the photos into her laptop. As she and Kia stepped through the pictures, they made an ugly discovery. Not only had the original murder image returned to the series of photos, but a second, totally new, photo of an entirely different murder had found its way into the series.

"You damned well better come over after school to see the images for yourself," Kia said. "I'll leave the office early." At promptly three o'clock Sam arrived. She again started in on him. He tried unsuccessfully to calm her down. Even worse, Peggy refused to see her father. He could hear her sobbing behind the closed door of her room.

He sat down at the laptop as it booted up on the dining room table. The second crime scene filled the screen. Another woman, propped up against a brass headboard…a bloodless pillow this time behind her head…blonde…contorted face…multiple stab wounds…bloodstains on a yellow dress. Similar bedroom as in the first photo. Same staged look. He clicked on "data," and sure enough, he found the time set at 10:45 p.m. and the date 10.10.13.

"Sam, this is totally bizarre," said Kia. "Today is Wednesday the ninth. Thursday the tenth, hasn't happened yet. If this is another one of your unholy pranks, I'll get a court order to cancel all your visitations. How dare you bring this kind of trash into our house—into our lives?"

Sam had had enough. "Kia, gimme me a break. Have I ever played a prank of any kind on you or Peggy? That isn't like me, and you know it. I'm wondering whether someone else could have handled the camera or the new memory card. When you were in the park yesterday, was the camera left unattended for any length of time?"

"No!" she shot back. "Let me remind you that you were the one who left the camera outside our door."

Reluctantly, he nodded and admitted to himself, *How could I have been so stupid? I walked right into that one.* "Kia, I've said it before and I'm saying it again. I promise you I will get to the bottom of this." He asked her for a fresh paper bag, tucked the camera inside, and left.

At the kitchen table, Kia seethed, her normally cool demeanor unstrung. *How could this be happening?* She and Sam had met as juniors at Kaimuki High. He played basketball, a hotshot varsity forward for the Bulldogs. To Kia he'd been the sexiest, sweetest guy in the whole school. By senior year they were going steady. She was headed for college and law school. Sam went straight into the Honolulu Police Academy and they married right after his graduation. Soon after he joined the HPD, Kia's deep love and respect for him grew. As a police officer, he had a take-charge demeanor, and even now, with his enforced medical retirement, his instincts for leadership came into play.

Or did they? She shuddered. *Is everything falling apart?*

* * * *

When Sam returned to the Homicide unit, he found Mose and Danny going over the lab report on the ashen-faced brunette, the only body they'd recovered. From her fingerprints the woman was identified as one Vivian Koeller. Her prints were on file from a shoplifting offense in 2012. The medically estimated time of death was surprisingly close to the 11:23 p.m. time stamped on the photograph.

Uncanny! Sam thought. From all indications, the thirty-eight-year-old woman was struck on the back of the head with a blunt instrument and then stabbed five times. The head blow merely rendered the victim unconscious, while the stab wounds were the clincher. Apparently, the woman had protected, probably consensual, sex earlier that evening; no semen found. Five stabbings meant that the perp had killed in a rage.

Two officers, canvassing the neighborhood, found that the apartment was hers, and that she lived alone. She had regular visitors, but no one had ever noticed anyone in particular going in or out. The officers failed to find any useful correspondence, cell phone data, or telephone list.

"Nothing like a dead end," said the discouraged Danny, closing the file folder.

"Not so fast, my man," said Sam. "My daughter's camera has come up with another vicious photograph. And the first photo is back! Let's have a gander on the big screen. Maybe this new one is ready to reveal something more." He opened the camera and held out the flash memory card.

Danny looked startled. "Well, that's news." He inserted the card and transferred the second murder photo to his computer. Sam drew up a chair as the picture came into view.

The fully dressed woman on the screen appeared to be in

her late thirties or early forties. At least four major stab wounds were evident from the stains on the front of her muted yellow dress.

"The facial features are similar, almost like the two women were related. Even the bedroom could be the same, but that's unlikely because Vivian Koeller's crime scene has been sealed," said Danny. "I've even got a man there round the clock. This woman's also fully dressed. Rape doesn't seem likely."

"You're right," Sam said. "The clothes aren't in disarray in either photo. Plus, no signs of a struggle in either one."

"But do we have a serial killer here?" Danny asked. "There are enough similarities between the two murders to say one killer did both."

"I agree," said Sam. "Maybe we ought to focus on what's different between the two."

"Like what?" asked Danny.

"Like, there's no blood on the pillow in the second photo. Maybe there's no head trauma this time."

"They're pretty close in age—possibly only a few years apart," Mose said, speaking up for the first time. "What else is different?"

"Hair color," Sam noted. "One brunette, one blonde. The first one's a looker, the second's a bit thick around the waist and has a more manly face."

"Could it be the choices are random?" Danny suggested. "What about the annotation?"

"Just the time and date for tomorrow night," Sam said, checking to be sure nothing had changed. Nothing had.

"What about the camera?" Mose asked. "This is weird. It can't be some kind of magic that it knows when the murder will take place."

"Of course not," answered Sam. "The perp is playing with our heads. I guess we'll have to babysit the phone tomorrow night."

"Hey!" Danny retorted. "What's this *we* business, buddy?

It only takes *one* to answer the phone. You know where to find me."

Sam nodded. "Yeah, sure." The reminder hurt. He was just a cabbie now. And that was never going to change.

Danny re-copied the memory card data onto a thumb drive memory and locked it away before sending the suspect camera to Lou Grossa in the photo lab to search for mechanical tampering or firmware anomalies. He made copies of the new photo and distributed them as he had done two nights earlier.

That night Sam sat down at his own computer and went online to order a new birthday camera for Peggy. It would be a step up from the first one and a different brand. But after a few moments of browsing, he stopped and shut down his machine. He had a better idea.

* * * *

Thursday morning Lou Grossa walked into the Homicide squad room. He was the camera maven in the Crime Lab's Photo Unit. Danny had filled him in on the forensics of the murder, as well as the second photo phenomenon.

"The camera works perfectly," Lou reported. "The operating program is driven from a programmable read-only memory type that cannot be reprogrammed."

"Couldn't an alternate device be substituted?" asked Sam. He'd been listening from the open door and now ski-walked in uninvited.

"I saw no signs of re-soldering on this circuit board," replied Lou.

"Maybe someone substituted a different board," said Danny.

"Not very likely," said Lou. "The board is a factory original, and even if it wasn't, there's still the problem of re-programming. It would take special programming equipment and a blank virgin device manufactured just for this camera maker."

"What about the memory card?" asked Sam.

"Nothing unusual there," said Lou. "Still pristine: sixty-four megabytes and every bit functional. I copied the contents and ran some tests. It's a standard replacement for the sixteen-megabyte card shipped with the camera."

"But couldn't the card be removed and altered?" Sam pressed.

"Of course," said Lou. "That's what it's designed to do. But in this case, the card was brand-new. It couldn't be removed and reinserted as many times as you said without showing some signs of wear. If the camera is as new as you say, the mating connector for the card shows much more wear than the card itself."

"In plain English, please?" Danny piped up.

"It means that more than one memory card has been used in this camera."

Sam's fingers ruffled his thick black hair as he shook his head in disbelief. His brown eyes smoldered with frustration and his broad shoulders slumped visibly. "How could someone insert bootlegged pictures into a series of photographs that someone else took?"

"Simple," said Lou. "Dump the card's pictures into any laptop, add the extra picture, and edit the series order. Then dump the pictures back onto the memory card."

"Holy crap!" Danny said.

"Anything else unusual?" asked Sam.

"Yeah," said Lou, "but I can't quite put my finger on it. There were a few areas on the picture that seemed a little fuzzy when I enlarged the screen by 200 percent. But I couldn't determine any tampering at that size."

"Thanks, Lou," Danny said.

"Thanks from me too, Lou," Sam added. "You've been a great help."

Lou left and headed back to his lab.

Sam wanted a look at the enlarged photos one more time, so Danny slid the memory card into his desktop computer. They waited for the screen to come alive. Meanwhile, Sam wracked his brain, trying to remember all the times he'd left the camera unattended and who might have had access. The screen came alive, all right, but as soon as the operating system finished regenerating, the screen turned blue, then filled with black running error messages and, finally, reset to restart the wake-up process.

The machine recycled on its own for several minutes before Danny shut it down and tried again with the same result. "Damn!" He slapped the side of the computer case with a vengeance. Swiveling around in his chair, he said, "I've got another idea, pal." Unlocking the top drawer of his desk, Danny removed the thumb drive memory containing both photos and strode over to his partner's unoccupied station. "Mose won't be in 'til two," he said. Sam hobbled close behind and lowered himself into a chair from the side of the desk.

Mose's computer came up briskly. Danny shoved the thumb drive memory into the front panel USB port and used the mouse to reach Mose's photo files. He was about to download them when he noticed a file folder labeled "SAM." The two men looked at each other.

"Open it," Sam said.

Danny didn't need to be told. Adjusting his wire-rimmed glasses, he leaned forward, his body on alert. He opened the folder to find a whole series of photo files. Switching to thumbnail views gave the two of them quite a shock.

"Whoa!" Sam bellowed. "What the hell?"

"Yeah," Danny said. "This is not good."

They recognized all of the nature photos and the two sinister shots from Peggy's camera. There were more photos in the computer folder. Apparently, some of the remaining photos were used to doctor the two sinister ones. There were even a few magazine clippings that might have found their way into the doctoring mix.

Danny turned to Sam. "Obviously, those two rogue photos were doctored on this computer."

Sam's brain launched into overdrive as he thought back to the beginning of his investigation. He correlated Mose Kauahi's presence in the office with the moments that he himself had carelessly left the birthday camera unattended. *Jeez,* he thought. *All for a candy bar and to schmooze.* Much of it fit—too much. Mose could even have followed him to Kia's front door.

Heavy footsteps woke him from his thoughts. He turned to face Mose, who dropped into the chair at an adjacent desk.

"So now you know everything, *Detective,*" said Mose with a sneer. "I should have known I couldn't put anything past my old partner. But somehow I had to try."

Sam's strong ruddy face turned redder yet as he struggled for control. "What was Vivian Koeller to you? And that other woman too?"

"There was no other woman...only Vivian." Mose leaned back, legs splayed out, the very picture of relaxation. "Vivian had run away from some horse farm over on the Big Island, near Waimea. Being broke, she needed a place to stay for the night, so I bought her a motel room. She was grateful, and one thing led to another."

"And you, being big-hearted, obliged. Where'd you meet her?" asked Sam.

"At Charlie's. You were there that night, only you went home early. It was just a fling at first, and then I couldn't give it up. I wasn't harming anyone, and the poor kid was one helluva lay."

"Harming anyone?" Sam burst out. "What about your Annie? You were throwing fifteen years of marriage in the garbage for a piece of flesh?"

By now the confrontation and casual confession had attracted the attention of other detectives at their desks—shuffling papers or holding cell phones to their ears, but listening keenly. Neither Sam nor Mose seemed to care. In fact, Danny was thinking, *the more who hear the better.*

Mose continued. "I told Annie I was taking extra computer graphics courses. Photoshop and stuff."

"Right," Sam said. "Annie's a sweet woman, too good for the likes of you, and a swell mom to Junior. You were throwing all that out the window?"

"Of course not," replied Mose. "I thought I'd play until I tired of Vivian, and Annie would never find out."

"So what happened that turned you into a killer?"

"Vivian kept needling me to dump Annie and hook up with her permanently. Well, sir, that wasn't going to happen, so I tried ending the affair. But she wasn't having any of it. She began screaming at me and pounding on me with her fists, so I smacked her one across the face. I guess I hit the bitch too hard. Her head snapped back, and she fell, hitting her head on the dresser."

"Is that when you stabbed her five times?" Sam asked, unable to hide his disgust.

"No! No! I didn't mean to kill her, at least not then. At first I thought I'd only knocked her out, so I picked her up and laid her on the bed. I didn't notice the blood in her hair until it stained the pillow. She was still breathing okay, but didn't regain consciousness."

Danny's eyes narrowed. "Then what?"

"I began to realize the full impact of what I'd done and what could happen to the rest of my life. My marriage, my career, my pension, and if she died I'd have to serve some time. I saw my whole life going down the toilet. The way I saw it I had three choices. One, I could turn myself in and get at least five years for manslaughter and lose Annie and my son in the process. Two, I could finish the job, clean the place up, and walk away like nothing ever happened. I don't think anyone ever saw us together, but any reasonable detective work would focus on the disgruntled lover. This left choice three. I could walk away, but I needed to divert attention to another motive. That's when I got the whole serial killer idea."

"So you decided to mess with *my mind and my daughter's?* Why? We've always been pals—partners, for God's sake. And what did my little kid ever do to you?"

"Not a damned thing," said Mose. "It was just a great way to introduce the serial killer diversion. But you, Sam. You were lording it over me, ordering me around from the day you made sergeant—right up until the time you got shot. You even wrote me up when you found me drinking on the job. It cost me a month's pay and any decent shot I'll ever have at making sergeant."

Sam shook his head. "Hell, I couldn't cover for you then and you knew it."

Danny had heard enough. "You damned fiend. Tell me where the other body is."

"It doesn't exist," said Mose with a boyish, how-clever-I-am grin on his face. "I created it by re-pixelizing several photographs. I created a new face, changed the hair and dress color, and added gory details to the original high-resolution photograph. You should try Photoshop sometime. It works great."

Sam scowled. "Enough with the sarcasm. But how did you manage to insert a death photo of Vivian two days before she actually died? Her body was still warm when we found her."

"I took the original photo while she was still alive, but unconscious," Mose answered. "Don't ask me why I took the picture. I just did."

"You mean you didn't have the decency to get the poor girl any medical attention while she was still alive?" broke in a very agitated Danny.

"And instead you stabbed her five times?" raged Sam.

"Not right away. I left her and came back two days later and stabbed her. At first I wasn't sure what to do. She was barely alive when I put the blade to her. She would have died anyway."

After several moments of stunned silence, Sam asked, "And you needed to doctor the faces too? How devious can one man get?"

"I simply added the pixelized wounds from cold-case files. And last Sunday I saw the camera you bought for Peggy on top of the file cabinet. I loaded the first nine slots of a virgin memory card with the first crime scene photo, and then erased the first eight slots to make them available to the user. You'd be amazed how often you made that gift camera available to me. I did the second picture exactly the same way."

47

"That's not the *how* I meant, you creep, and you know it. Don't you have any regrets?" asked Sam. "After all, you took a human life."

"Sam, I swear it was an accident. The first part, anyway. Then I completely panicked. If the bitch lived, she would have ruined my life. I'm sorry for the whole affair and how it turned out."

"Sure you are. I can hear the remorse in your voice," Sam said. "You had two whole days to think about it before she actually died. You could have changed your mind and called for help at any time. That's premeditated murder in my book. And by the way, I'm curious. How did you manage to get the original picture into Peggy's camera before I even gave it to her?"

"You've been talking about her birthday present for more than a month. It fell right into my plan. When you called me for drinks on Saturday night, you said you wanted to show off the new camera. I just brought the altered memory card along to Charlie's. I made the switch when you went to the head."

Sam looked stricken. "I had no idea you hated me that much."

Danny stood up. "Some partner you turned out to be, Mose. You should have taken your medicine. You could have served a few years for manslaughter and possibly even survived your marriage. Now you're facing charges of murder in the first degree."

Mose straightened up, stood, and unclipped the handcuffs from his belt. He held them out to Sam. "You can do the honors, old buddy."

A deeply saddened ex-detective placed the cuffs on his former partner's wrists.

Danny grabbed Mose by the arm and nudged him toward the elevator—to booking. Then to the basement lockup.

* * * *

Sam knew he couldn't rest until he'd made things right with Peggy and her mother. He got permission to visit the following afternoon. First, he gently sent his daughter to her room. Then, for

48

more than an hour, he described every detail of his former partner's crimes.

Finally, Kia responded, her eyes filled with remorse. "Mose? Your partner? Such a betrayal. I'm sorry, Sam. So sorry I doubted you." She called to Peggy to join them.

Her father related a limited, sanitized version. Peggy crawled onto his lap and gave him a hug.

"Hey, Peggs," he said, adding a bear hug of his own. "How about coming to my place for a sleepover?"

"Okay, Daddy, but I'll only come if Goldie can sleep in my room with me."

Sam grinned. "Fine with me. If it's okay with your mother, of course."

Kia broke into a happy smile, the first in many days.

But Sam wasn't quite through. He pulled out his wallet and drew out a bunch of twenties. Handing them to his ex-wife, he said, "Our daughter needs a new camera. My gift, of course. But this time it's out of my hands. Literally."

She laughed and took the bills.

§

Episode Four
The Getaway Cab

THIS PARTICULAR MONDAY AFTERNOON FOUND SAM DRIVING down South King Street with his partner harnessed as usual beside him. Just past the corner of King and Punahou, Goldie let out a sharp yip, scratched at her door handle, and leaned out her window. She'd seen a man frantically trying to flag them down. Alerted, Sam eased toward the curb, pulled into an empty parking space, and gave him the once-over—neatly dressed in a sport shirt and dark pants. He looked like he could afford the fare. Sam had been burned that way recently. The tall, trim *haole* slid into the back seat and slammed the door shut.

"Where to, brah?" Sam asked briskly.

"Kaimuki! And get a move on!"

"Any particular address?" Sam queried.

"Yah! 554 Sixth Avenue, but…" the man added in a voice now tinged with tension, "you can let me out at the corner of Sixth and Wai'alae. I got some shopping to do. Yah?"

"Sure thing!" said Sam. He powered away from the curb and nosed the cab into the lane for the eastbound freeway ramp. A glance in the rear-view mirror revealed the stranger gripping his blue gym bag for dear life. Sam also got a second look. The man had put on sunglasses with almost black lenses. His fair-skinned head was completely bald. He had a thick, light-brown mustache, the tips drooping to the edges of his mouth, and a clipped goatee.

Several blocks later, Sam braked slightly when he saw a turmoil of activity in front of Oceanic National Bank: two police cruisers, a shiny black SUV, and a crowd of onlookers. Although the cabbie's days as a detective were over, he could still put two and two together.

But a lot of good it did him. The next thing he felt was a cold gun barrel pressed a half-inch into the back of his neck. The strapping thirty-eight-year-old Hawai'ian now had to face the grim truth: even in his new life, trouble always found him anyway.

"Keep driving, sucker, or you're one dead dude, yah?"

Sam's large-knuckled hands tightened on the steering wheel. *What the hell? The guy looked legit at the curb. How could I have been so wrong?* The cab kept rolling on its current course. He swore under his breath.

Goldie was a companion of few words. But even without a vocabulary, she quickly perceived the situation and struggled against her leather restraining harness. She began to growl and bark intermittently, trying to get at the stranger's wrist—smartly kept just out of her reach. The barrel of a revolver now pointed in her direction.

"No, no! Don't hurt her," cried Sam. "I'll take you wherever you need to go. Honest! I won't try anything funny."

"Then make her stop that damned racket." The passenger kept his gun pointed at the dog. Sam stole another glance at his fare: the impenetrable dark glasses and the goatee, which ended an inch below the man's chin, giving him a fierce, even satanic, look.

Keeping his left hand on the wheel, Sam held up one finger of his right hand in Goldie's direction, the signal to stop growling at non-tipping fares. She reluctantly gave up the cause and tilted her head questioningly at Sam, who said, "Stop it, girl. Easy now."

"And while you're at it," the passenger snapped, "hand me that smart phone off the dashboard."

Oh crap, the lifeline to my business. Sam pulled it out of its clip and did as he was told.

"Now, buster, both hands on the wheel or you lose one fine dog."

"Sure, sure, anything you say, man."

Satisfied, the stranger leaned back in the seat and rested the elbow of his gun hand on the armrest while still training the weapon on Goldie. The quieted retriever still didn't trust him. She turned as far as her harness would allow and managed to keep staring at him, making an obviously agitated man even more so. The fare tried to look away, but couldn't. The dog was too prominent a distraction. He shoved the gun in her face, but that only elicited a single bark.

"Tell her to stop staring at me or she's a goner."

"Goldie!" Sam scolded, yanking her harness around with his free hand so that she faced front. Without the weapon, the scene would've been comical.

The cab left South King, entered the H-1 freeway, and sped toward the Sixth Avenue exit to take the passenger to Kaimuki. But when Sam moved into the far-right lane, the emboldened passenger gruffly announced, "No, forget it, don't get off. Keep going."

"I thought you—"

"This piece sez I'm doing the thinking in this here cab. Stay on H-1 'til I tell you to get off. Yah?" The man's movements became jerky and his speech ping-ponged between school English and pidgin. He leaned forward to push the revolver barrel against Sam's neck, then slouched back once more.

"Yeah, I get you." Sam began to have visions of being mugged and rolled for his paltry cashbox contents and left somewhere in a ditch in the boonies. Or worse yet, separated from Goldie or killed. Not so much for himself, but he feared for his dog. And, of course, there was no hope of this hoodlum paying his fare, even though the meter now showed $16.50 and climbing.

As Sam drove past Kāhala Mall, the freeway became the Kalaniana'ole Highway and the scenery more residential. "Where are we headed?" he asked when the meter now showed $38. "A hideaway maybe?"

"Don't know. I'll tell you when I git it all figured out. Meanwhile, butt out. Yer dog too!"

"You mean you stuck up a big-time bank and didn't have any idea of a getaway? An escape plan of some sort?" Sam looked up at the mirror and cracked a wry smile.

"Yah, it was kinda sudden. You know, an impassive kinda thing."

"You mean impulsive, unplanned?"

"Yah, that's it, impulsive. It seemed like the only solution. And you kin wipe that silly smirk off yer puss. Hey, why you slowing down, clown?"

"You don't want a cop stopping me for running a red light, do you?"

"Right! Good thinking. But don't get cute. And don't let me hear any more of your English lessons."

Sam rolled up to the light and stopped. Upscale homes lined the highway, many with imposing gates or walls and attached two-car garages. As the light turned green, the passenger ordered, "Keep going, but slower. I'm lookin' for something." And half a mile later, "Hey, take that street and follow it around." Sam made a sharp left, then slowed to a crawl, creeping along, turning and winding where instructed.

"See that house at the end of the street? Turn in there."

Even before they reached the property, Sam could tell it was an anomaly in the neighborhood of luxury homes: a modest stucco ranch, faded green. As the cab approached, Sam spotted the FOR SALE sign posted on the front lawn and a lockbox on the doorknob. The lawn looked recently mowed, but with scattered patches of dried grass from lack of watering. *Odd when you're trying to sell,* he thought. Real estate agents always harped on the need for curb appeal. A cluster of potted white azaleas to the left of the front door looked healthy, as if they'd come straight from a garden center.

"Pull into this driveway," the passenger ordered, "and keep going all the way to the back."

The long, narrow, cement driveway had tufts of grass poking up through the cracks. *This is bad,* Sam realized. *No parked cars.*

Probably no one home. We'll be out of sight of the street. At the rear of the house he braked in front of an empty one-car carport, next to a small bleak yard.

"Into the carport, bub. Turn off your engine, leave the keys in the ignition, and stay where you are, hands on the wheel." The passenger left the back seat, one fist clutching his prized gym bag, and walked the twenty feet sideways to the back door, continuing to point his weapon in Goldie's direction.

Inside Sam's powerful chest his heart pounded painfully. As a cabbie, he and Goldie had never been physically threatened. *Now this son-of-a-bitch. Bank robber. Kidnapper. Armed. Why didn't he just hijack my cab and leave us out on the street?* Sam mentally rehearsed an idea of escape. *I'd have to reverse at least twice to get out of this carport and turn around. Or back out all the way to the street. Too slow. Too many opportunities for the guy to shoot the tires out, or worse yet, us.*

In the late afternoon sun, sweat gleamed on the gunman's bald head as he used the barrel of the revolver to punch through the nylon fabric of the screen door. He released the hook and eye securing it. Still holding the gun, swinging it every few seconds in the general direction of the cab, he peeked inside the house through the window in the upper half of the storm door. He tried the doorknob. It was locked. Grabbing the gun barrel, he slammed the grip into the glass pane, then ran the barrel around the perimeter of the broken pane to clear the shards. Reaching in, he released both deadbolt and button in the knob. The door swung open. He approached the car once more, pointing the gun at Sam. "Leave the keys in the ignition and get out."

Still in dark glasses, the gunman loomed over the driver's window and scowled. Deep vertical creases split his smooth brow. "No funny business now. And bring the mutt too. Don't want her barking and alerting all the neighbors."

Oh rats! Sam thought as he released Goldie's harness. Fearing his canine partner's reckless bravado, Sam clipped the leash onto her collar so he could restrain her when he needed to. He undid the heavy-duty twist-tie that held Cane and Able vertically

54

against the dashboard and slowly hoisted himself out of the cab.

The gunman stepped back, realizing that the canes could also be used as weapons, but from his perspective, they did keep Sam's hands in constant view. He motioned Sam and Goldie to walk ahead of him toward the back door. "Get going, brah! Stop wasting my time. Into the kitchen!"

Sam jerked to a stop before they approached the door. Shards of glass littered the patio flagstones. Supporting himself on his canes, he swept one foot from side to side to clear the shards away before they could lodge themselves into Goldie's tender paws. The impatient revolver pressing against his back nudged him forward through the kitchen door. His canine pal followed.

The kitchen had an antiseptic cleanser smell as well as a new-ish quality, most likely scrubbed and fitted out for selling. The granite counter and shiny appliances looked like they'd been recently installed. Sam's gut churned. *What the hell are we doing here?* He found out soon enough. The gunman dropped the heavy gym bag on the counter. Then he flung open the double doors to the under-sink cabinet and instructed Sam to tie his dog to the drain plumbing underneath. Sam undid the leash while holding Goldie between his legs. He passed the leash clip around the drain trap and through the leash's loop handle before clipping it back on Goldie's collar. She strained against the futility of the tether, then flopped down on the tile floor, resorting to a low, frustrated whine.

"Now face the wall," the gunman commanded. "Over there," he pointed with the revolver.

Sam took a few steps and turned to face the blank white wall, pressing down on his canes to support his upper body weight. Just as his eyes lit on a wall phone a few feet to his left, the gunman's left hand reached out and ripped the connecting cord from its innards. Not daring to turn around, Sam listened. He could hear rummaging through many of the kitchen drawers and cabinets, followed by an "Ah" of satisfaction. But the gun barrel's steel returned, this time to incite searing pain into the small of his back.

"Move!" the gunman ordered. His shove sent Sam into the dining room.

Sam took in his new surroundings. *For a small home, quite grandly furnished, unlike the seedy yard*, he thought. A breakfront held fancy china. A credenza sported Southwest glazed pottery. Four high-back chairs, upholstered in brocade, accompanied an oval dining table. Then Sam suddenly realized: *The possessions—the current residents haven't moved out yet. That family could be in real danger if they return home too soon.*

Flanking the bay window on the driveway side of the house were two matching side chairs with arms. They had a formal, somewhat fragile, look: graceful black wood frames, round backs, and beige linen upholstery. Another bruising nudge against Sam's back moved him toward one of these chairs, where he was ordered to sit. He laid the canes against the adjacent one and sat down obediently.

Sam soon learned what the prized kitchen discovery was. The gunman produced a large roll of silver duct tape and instructed the cabbie to tape his own right wrist to the chair's arm. Sam picked at the tape end until it was free. He laid his right arm down on the chair arm, and stretched the tape loosely over his wrist, binding it with two complete wraps.

"Three times around," the gunman ordered. "Tight too."

At that point Sam seriously considered: *What if I stand up quickly and round-house this guy with the chair? Nope, too heavy, too awkward, too risky. My reflexes just aren't that fast anymore. I'd get myself killed. Maybe Goldie too.*

Reading his thoughts, the gunman laid the revolver down on the table. He grabbed the roll from Sam, and roughly continued the job himself, taping Sam's left wrist to the left chair arm. Next the gunman taped each of his shins to the individual chair legs. As an afterthought, he added a few turns to Sam's forearms and a strip across his mouth, then disappeared back into the kitchen. Sam could hear him rummaging around again. A barrage of choice words accompanied the opening and closing of the refrigerator door, indicating, perhaps, the lack of anything to eat. *If the fridge is empty, maybe the family moved out*, Sam reasoned.

The next thing he heard was the screen door banging, followed a few moments later by a familiar car door slamming shut. *The SOB's taking my cab.* Out of the corner of one eye he saw a flash of yellow pass by the window as his taxi returned to the street.

Icy pools of sweat collected in Sam's hairy armpits and trickled down his bare skin under his polo shirt while he tried to figure out the gunman's next moves. *Either he's leaving us like this to rot or he's gone to get food. If it's for food, I've got maybe twenty or thirty minutes to get us out of this mess. But how?*

The wide duct tape pressed across his mouth was making it hard for him to breathe through his nose, especially with his chronic sinus condition. The tape wrapping his arms and wrists was cutting into his flesh. He tested the flexibility of his bonds, but the tight taping had left no slack for movement between his wrists and elbows.

Refusing to panic, Sam Nahoe now considered his own vulnerability. *If I'm a goner, what happens to little Peggy and Kia? Maybe I was too hasty agreeing to our divorce. God, was I that tough to live with? Yeah, I was. If I die here, they shouldn't want for anything, what with my disability pension, my social security, and Kia's law practice. Hey, wait a minute! If the bastard intended to kill Goldie and me, why bother tying us up? It would've been simpler to just shoot us right off the bat. Perhaps he plans to hole up here for a few days. Not likely. He must know the family could be coming back. Besides, the house is on the market. Real estate agents will be bringing buyers. What if he's headed for the airport to get off the island? Nah. This guy is no professional. Maybe he left the gym bag in the kitchen. I wonder how much money's in it. How much he forced from a teller. Hell, I can't stay here helpless forever. What happens when I gotta pee? I've got to try something to get loose. And fast.*

Sam started by testing the durability of the chair. He shifted his 240-pound bulk left and right, then rocked back and forth until he heard a few encouraging creaks. He'd been annoyed with himself for putting on twenty pounds since he left HPD, but at this moment, the extra weight was working for him. That and knowing he had built considerable upper body muscle during his rehab and with his continuing twice-a-week gym workouts. Sam applied all his forearm strength inward, then outward, repeating the motion—until a glue joint at the rear of the left chair arm came free and the front of it splintered downward. Now he applied the power of both his forearms to the right arm of the chair. Crack! It gave way. If the gunman had merely bound his wrists, he doubted whether he would have had the leverage and strength to achieve this much. The two small chair arms remained attached to his forearms like splints. They also added a degree of clumsiness to his every movement.

He tried picking at the tape ends with the opposite hand using his fingernails, but it proved tedious and he knew time was of the essence. He had something more urgent to do. He lowered his head until his face met his fingers. Awkwardly, he peeled off the duct tape sealed across his mouth, and took several deep breaths of relief.

Each of his legs was still taped to each front chair leg. He leaned forward until he could reach out to touch the table. With his taped hands and then a few inches to the right, the chair tilted with him. He placed a good portion of his weight on the right chair leg by re-positioning himself. The leg cracked at the glue joint. He flopped to the floor as the chair fell over, but the right chair leg did not break; it only bent at a slight angle.

He had to try again. He could hear the wall clock in the kitchen, each loud tick a warning of precious seconds lost. Sitting on the floor, anchoring both hands on the edge of the table, he chinned himself until he could wrestle first one splinted forearm and then the other up to the tabletop. Leaning on one elbow, he used the opposite wrist to push down, lifting himself enough to drag the chair seat underneath him once more.

At the pinnacle of stress he howled in pain. The splint had stabbed his underarm. Hearing his cry from the kitchen, Goldie replied with a worried yelp of her own and started straining against the plumbing with renewed fervor.

Allowing several minutes for precariously resting, or rather balancing, in the cockeyed chair, Sam readied himself for the second try. This time the leg broke free! Now he was able to move one of his own legs independently from the other. He limped and dragged what was left of the attached chair into the kitchen. As he expected, the gun was gone. He itched to open the gym bag. Just how much money had the SOB gotten away with? But he didn't dare take the time.

Goldie joyously lurched toward him, tearing the U-shaped drain trap from the rest of the plumbing under the kitchen cabinet. Water puddled and squirted out, discharging an acrid smell of sewer gases. Goldie's nails scratched the tile floor as she gained traction and loped to him, with the U-trap clanging and bouncing behind her.

"Good girl!" Sam said. "Now lie down!" In the third most likely drawer, he found a nine-inch serrated knife. He had to get rid of the wood chair pieces cutting into his flesh. Working on the left arm with his right hand, he began sawing through the duct tape on the chair arm side to avoid cutting himself. Once through the length of forearm tape, he rolled the wood arm away—slowly peeling the tape away from his bare skin, and along with it, tufts of his own curly black hairs. He repeated the process for the second arm and then for both legs. Panting from the exertion, he scooped up all the ragged chair limbs, limped back into the dining room, and threw them into the far corner behind the breakfront, where the gunman wouldn't see them.

Next he limped around the table to retrieve his canes. Ski-walking down the hall, with the irrepressible Goldie clanging close behind, he found the master bedroom. He hoped to locate a second serviceable phone there. "Bingo!" he said aloud, spotting the landline phone on the nearest nightstand.

Punching in 9-1-1, he reached HPD headquarters and his friend Detective Sergeant Aiden Harada in Robbery, and told him as much as he could as fast as he could. Aiden said he would alert the FBI and send out the nearest local police response. "Better approach without a siren," Sam cautioned. "You don't want to frighten him away if you get here before he returns. And remember, he's armed." No sooner had Sam set the receiver down when he heard his cab coming up the long driveway.

Shaking from exhaustion, he grabbed Cane and Able and ski-walked back down the hall and into the kitchen with Goldie clanging right behind him. He tossed the leash loop and U-trap into the under-sink cabinet and closed the door on the leash so that Goldie still looked tied up as before.

The cab door slammed shut. Sam set his canes against the counter, grabbed the serrated knife, and hid behind the kitchen door. He waited. Minutes passed. The screen door squeaked open. Goldie's head jerked up. She stood, her whole retriever body frozen on alert. The storm door opened—with their captor's gun arm extended. He stepped into the kitchen, cradling a large grocery bag in his other arm. From Sam's hiding place, his stomach gurgled out of control. The gunman turned toward the sound.

Goldie lunged toward him, popping open the cabinet door and dragging the noisy U-trap behind her. The startled gunman dropped his bag of groceries and pivoted toward her. Sam reached out from behind the door and slashed the man's extended bare arm all the way from the elbow down to the wrist. The revolver fell to the floor. Sam kicked it out of the way. He dove at the screaming man, slamming him against the wall. There they struggled and exchanged a half-dozen short jabs. The man howled and went for Sam's eyes with two fingers, but Sam grabbed that threatening wrist in time and wrenched the elbow with his other hand in a move that flipped his opponent around to face the wall. Sam wrestled him to the floor in front of the sink by twisting his good arm behind him. Kneeling on the man's legs, Sam unclipped Goldie's leash and used it to lash the twisted arm to the back of his prisoner's belt.

Goldie, overjoyed to be free of the leash and plumbing pipe, placed her front paws on the man's shoulders to help. Sam had trained her well.

"Git that damn dog off me!" Their prisoner was lying with his head to one side, spitting and sputtering from her shaggy fur covering his mouth.

"Down, Goldie!" Sam commanded, breathing hard, but laughing while she retreated.

Struggling, the bank robber rolled over onto his back. "Hey,

60

man, you gonna let me bleed to death?"

Still one arrogant dirtbag, thought Sam. "Maybe I should, the way you left us. What do you think of that, wise guy? Should we help him, girl?"

Goldie let loose a short high-pitched bark.

Sam grinned. "I'll take that as a yes."

By now blood was spreading across the floor, mixing with the putrid drain water. Sam pulled several dish towels off a rack above the sink, wrapped them around the knife wound, and secured them in place with the lengths of duct tape he'd cut from his legs and arms. "That should hold you for now," he said. "And this too." He added two turns of tape around both the perp's ankles.

Sam suddenly remembered: he'd been forced to hand over his smart phone in the cab. *He's probably got it on him.* He found it in a pants pocket and called for an ambulance. Physically drained, he grabbed his canes, half-staggered to the front door, and unlocked it, leaving it wide open. Then he hobbled back to the kitchen. Goldie trotted close behind, fearing danger was still with them.

Two uniformed officers arrived first and burst through the open front door with their guns drawn. "Police! Toss out your weapons and you won't get hurt."

"All clear, Officers," Sam called to them. "I've got the turkey trussed up in the kitchen—ready for the oven, but he'll need some medical attention first."

One officer entered through the dining room, yelling, "Clear!" The second one came down the hall from the bedrooms and entered the kitchen from the opposite direction. Doing a double-take when he saw Sam, he asked, "Hey, aren't you that detective from Homicide?"

"I used to be him," admitted Sam. "Now I'm just a plain solid citizen whose Checker Cab got hijacked, along with my partner here. That's my cab out back." He went on to provide more details. Just as Sam finished telling the story, Aiden Harada arrived at the same time as the ambulance and two FBI agents, who took charge of the gym bag.

As the EMTs attended to the bloody, swelling forearm, Aiden pulled the perp's wallet out of a hip pocket, studied the driver's license, and read him his Miranda rights.

"Wallace Macklenburg, you're under arrest for armed bank robbery, carjacking, kidnapping, assault with a deadly weapon, and who knows what else? You have the right to remain silent…"

The weakened Wallace still managed to spit out, "Screw you, cops, and you too, you friggin' cabbie. My life is ruined."

Aiden shook his head. "Can you believe this guy?"

In the dining room, the FBI agents had upended the gym bag and spread the bills out on the table. Sam just had to know. "How much cash was in there, anyway?"

"About five thousand bucks," one agent reported.

Aiden faced Wallace. "Hey, guy, you're gonna spend the rest of your pathetic life in prison for five thousand bucks."

The ambulance carrying Wallace sped away, accompanied by a police officer. Sam knew he himself would be heading down to headquarters to make a complete statement. His heart had begun subsiding to its normal rhythm as he studied the mess in the kitchen and dining room. He knew there was going to be a heap of explaining to do to the homeowners, not to mention cleaning and repairs.

What the hell, it's all in a day's work, although not exactly what I had in mind when I took to the road this morning. Maybe it's time for me to take the private investigator exam. Goldie and I keep running into trouble like it's a magnet or something. Why not get paid for it?

But where was Goldie? Not hard to find amid sounds of a rustling paper bag. She'd discovered the gunman's deli groceries strewn across the kitchen floor, and was rewarding herself with salami slices. With smudges of potato salad decorating her nose, she cocked her head and looked up at her partner, as if to ask:

"What? No pickle?"

§

Episode Five
High Stakes in Honolulu

SAM SAT IN THE BARE-BONES WAITING ROOM WITH TWO other men. Squirming a little in the hard-backed chair, he assumed they were there for the same reason: applying for a private investigator license.

With his stellar years at HPD, including commendations and a promotion, he assumed that confirmation would be a snap. He had breezed through the ninety-minute written exam of eighty questions. The personal paperwork, on the other hand, covered a wide area. Certain subjects? Well, he didn't want to go there.

"Mr. Nahoe? Follow me, please."

Sam hoisted himself up, followed the secretary, and was shown to a seat in an office with pea-green walls and one window overlooking street traffic. A beveled wooden nameplate with gold letters revealed the interviewer's name, Frank L. Gleason. The fifty-ish man with a hooked nose sat across a large desk piled with file folders. His outstretched hand accepted the application paperwork from Sam.

Mr. Gleason scanned the pages and said, "That's strange."

"What's strange?" Sam asked, wondering what could possibly have gone wrong.

"You failed to answer the first question, Mr. Nahoe." He held up the top page for Sam to see. "Was there some reason for this?"

Sam looked down at the first personal-history question, "Where were you born?" and he was lulled into a momentary out-of-body memory trance. He had deliberately left that answer blank. To state it in writing had struck him as hopeless. Sadly, it took him to his unwanted past, like it or not.

"Mr. Nahoe, I asked you about your birth."

By now his forbidden past was ready to explode. "Yes, sir, it's like this. The warden at the Women's Community Correctional Center allowed my momma to have her baby in the hospital because she didn't want to have me inside the prison. My Auntie Momi told me I was born in Saint Francis Hospital Center here on O'ahu."

Mr. Gleason paused, then his voice softened. "The question only meant whether you were born here on O'ahu or on an outer island or on the Mainland. And if I may ask, why was your mother imprisoned?"

"My momma, Kaleki Nahoe, was serving a three-year sentence for embezzling money from the cash register at Quigley's Bake Shop where she worked. She was five months pregnant when they locked her up."

"So your father took care of you?"

"No." Sam shook his head vehemently. "That rotter, Lui Nahoe, took off as soon as he knew she was pregnant again with me. He must have left the islands, because I searched for him when I became a police detective. I was never able to find him."

"I suppose you were glad to have your mom back when she got out?"

Sam's steady gaze met Mr. Gleason's. "Actually, sir, she never did get out. Another inmate stabbed her with a shiv over a pack of cigarettes."

"I'm so sorry, Mr. Nahoe. I see you've had a tough time of it."

"Yes, sir."

Mr. Gleason continued to peruse the application with only

a scant question here and there. Finally, he said, "I see you had an exemplary record at HPD—two commendations and your gold shield before you were medically retired."

"Yes, sir!"

Gleason pointed to the two canes. "Don't you think those walking sticks will present a problem in your proposed line of work?"

"No, sir! I'm quite resourceful. Besides…" Sam smiled. "Who would suspect the hobbling me during surveillance work? And I do plan to stay away from trouble."

"Do you plan to carry a piece?"

"No, sir, but I do have a permit to carry one."

Frank Gleason picked up his pen and scribbled several lines in the white space on the front page of the application. He leaned back in his chair. "You'll receive your test results within five days, as well as the review board's decision when they meet later this week."

"That's it?"

"Yes, that's all for now. And good luck to you, Mr. Nahoe."

"Thank you, sir." Sam rose and left the office feeling a bit uncertain.

* * * *

Six days later Sam and Goldie crept down Kalākaua Avenue through the heart of Waikīkī in their yellow Checker Cab, seeking one more fare for this Saturday night. Posted next to his taxi license was his brand-new private investigator's license. He had aced the exam. The letter had arrived only yesterday with the license inside. He had even picked out a dashboard frame to display it.

"Rrruff!" Goldie barked as they crawled through Waikīkī. Safely harnessed in her usual shotgun seat, she was doing what Sam had trained her to do: spot the waving arms of potential fares.

Sam saw a woman in a spaghetti-strapped black mini-dress waving them down in front of an ABC Store. Two roll-around suitcases were parked next to her eye-catching figure. The taxi screeched to a halt. Her bare arms revealed well-defined biceps. Long legs revealed the calf and thigh muscles of a woman who haunted the gym. Sam popped the trunk. She easily piled both pieces of luggage in and shut the lid.

"Where to, ma'am?" Sam asked, as she settled herself into the back seat.

No response.

He twisted halfway around to face his passenger. Thick curls of aggressively dyed red hair fell around the woman's unsmiling face. Deep lines of anger radiated from her generous mouth, spoiling the exotic image.

Still awaiting her response, he said, "Ma'am? Where're we going?"

"I don't know!" she burst out. Suddenly embarrassed, amid a flood of tears she said, "I haven't figured it out yet." Sam shrugged, started the meter, and joined the line of one-way traffic. At the far end of Waikīkī he turned into an empty parking space near the zoo, stopped the cab, and shut down the meter.

"Maybe she'll open up and tell me what's wrong if I talk to her," he said aloud to Goldie.

"Sorry," the woman managed, overhearing him. "Give me a minute. I'm having a terrible time."

Sam unhooked his seatbelt so he could turn to face her more squarely. "Where're you from?" he tried. No answer. "What's your name?"

"Are you really a private detective?" she asked, eyeing his PI license.

"Absolutely, ma'am, and I used to be one of Honolulu's Finest. I know it's unusual, but my cab is my office. How can I help you?"

"I'm not sure you can, but I wasn't trying to be rude. My name is Maxine Fish, and we're here vacationing from Cleveland Park, Ohio."

"We? You and?"

"My husband, Duane Fish."

66

"So what's the problem?"

"My husband." She dabbed at her pale cheeks with a monogrammed handkerchief.

"You're really gonna have to explain that one to me," he replied.

"I will," she promised. "We got here with Lilly and Phil Tremane, friends from home, last Sunday for a two-week stay at the Surflyer Hotel. Duane and I agreed to this trip so we could heal our marriage. We've been going over some rough patches lately. You see, winning or losing, my husband likes to play cards, high-stakes cards. Our life has been a roller-coaster, riding the ups and downs of personal finance. The first few days here were wonderful, but on Wednesday afternoon Duane met this man at a bar and learned about a floating poker game that night. I begged him not to go, but he went anyway."

"Did he come back to the hotel that night?" Sam asked.

"Yeah, around 3:30 in the morning. Something must've happened at the game. My guess is he lost a bundle. He didn't get up till noon Thursday, refused to shave or even take a shower, and then he snapped at me and our friends the whole rest of the day. The Tremanes aren't speaking to us now; they even moved to another hotel. Then, would you believe, at dinnertime Duane told me he was going back to the game that very night, and that's when we got into our biggest fight ever. He said he didn't give a damn what I wanted, he was going anyway."

"So you walked out on him," Sam prompted.

"Oh no. Duane walked out on me. It's been two days. He hasn't even called. I don't know where he is or how to find him. I have no idea if he ever intends to come back. But you know what? I'm not sure I want him back."

"So you're ready to go back to Ohio?" asked Sam.

"I thought so as I was coming out of the hotel, but now I'm not so sure. If I do leave, I might never know what happened to the bastard. Let's face it, he is my husband. I do care enough to find out if he's okay. And besides, if I just leave, what will I tell everybody back home?"

"What did you do with *his* things?" Sam asked.

"I left them in our room. Who knows, he might even go back there to crash or something. And if he doesn't, I'll let the hotel figure out what to do with his stuff when they discover that we're both gone."

Puzzled thoughts flew through Sam's brain. *Attired for traveling? Not exactly.* The mini-dress, and with her legs crossed, his eyes could hardly miss her shoes. Gleaming red stiletto heels with rhinestone-studded ankle straps.

"So…do you want me to find your missing husband or take you to the airport?"

"How much do you charge, Mr.—?" She strained to see his name on the license.

"Sam Nahoe. Call me Sam. It's forty-five to the airport and five hundred a day up front, plus expenses, to find errant husbands."

Maxine rummaged through her Prada hobo bag and pulled out a large paisley wallet. She slid ten ATM-crisp, $100 bills from it and handed them to Sam. "If you can't find him in two days, you can take me to the airport."

"Do you have a decent photo of Duane?" he asked, tucking away the bills with a tingle of satisfaction. *A client! And one who could spend a couple thousand bucks on a purse.*

She opened the wallet once more and extracted an arm-in-arm shot of the two of them. "This is from our last anniversary. Will that do?"

He studied the photo. "Yup!" The attractive couple stood in front of a restaurant, she all smiles, his smile rather stilted. Maxine, in a sparkly cocktail dress; Duane, in a brown sport jacket with a loose tie around his neck. Sam also noted the receding dark hair and assumed Duane was a bit older. "How tall is he and how much does he weigh?"

"He's five-nine, weighs about one-sixty."

"How old is he?"

"Forty-one."

"Did he mention where this game was?"

"All I heard was 'down the street.' "

"So where to now?" asked Sam. "Where do I drop you for the night, Mrs. Fish? Back to the hotel?"

"Call me Maxine. I'll be getting rid of the 'Mrs. Fish' real soon. Where? Someplace cheaper. Now that I'm on my own, I should be watching my cash flow."

"I can get you to a smaller hotel, or a Bed & Breakfast. Or better yet, I can take you to my Auntie Momi's place. She has two extra bedrooms that she rents by the week. Her last renter left on Monday, and she only charges a hundred-twenty bucks a night, meals included, if you eat whatever she cooks."

"Sounds like a deal made in heaven if she'll have me."

"She'll have you, all right. But first, you'll have to excuse Goldie and me while we take a little walk." Sam undid the harness, clipped on the short leash, and they exited the cab, Goldie's tail swaying as she hit the sidewalk. "My partner and me, we won't be more than a hundred yards away."

Maxine watched him. She liked the cabbie's broad back in the polo shirt, his taut-looking *tush,* and the stubborn determination in the way he walked, despite the canes. Her thoughts strayed. *He's a private investigator. Is he also a privates investigator?*

Returning in ten minutes, Sam clipped Goldie into her harness, started up the engine, and drove out onto Kapahulu Avenue, then H-1 west to Kalihi. Twenty minutes later they arrived at a freshly painted two-story house on a quiet, pleasant street. It didn't take long for Auntie Momi to adopt Maxine as one of her own. His auntie was like that.

* * * *

With mixed emotions, Sam decided to work that Sunday afternoon. Peggy had a birthday party to attend, so he might as well continue searching for Duane.

The Bottleneck Bar and Grill smelled of beer and bad breath. Sam was seeking out one of his favorite underworld snitches. He knew he'd find her here. She always set up shop in a back booth. And there she sat: Sleight-of-Hand Sophie Kalimalu, shuffling a deck of cards and cutting for high card and the money. The suckers never lasted long. She'd let them win a few hands before seriously cutting into their paychecks. Sam had to wait a while, sipping a ginger ale at the bar while she took a twenty-something to the cleaners. In the old days, as a cop, he'd permitted her to operate in return for high-quality street info. The dejected customer finally took his beer and departed, leaving his pride and money behind.

"Hi, Sophie," Sam said. "Howzit?" He slid into the booth and hooked Cane and Able over the top of the seat.

"Howzit yerself, Copper?" the robust, double-chinned woman answered. "Wait, I hear you drivin' a hack now, and anotha' thing. What's wit' dem giant chopsticks?"

"I've got some excess lead in my spine, giving me a giant-sized pain," Sam replied. "They help me get around."

"Ain't dat like havin' lead in your *'ōkole*?" Her rippling body flesh shook with silent laughter inside her ballooning floral mu'umu'u.

"That's exactly what it's like, my friend. What's going on, Sophie?"

"Wuddya want?" she asked, suddenly turning serious. "I ain't givin' you no more free stree' smar's. You ain't a lousy copper no more."

"I'm a private eye now, Sophie. And I've still got a lot of pull with the guys on the job. One call and they could shut you down plenty quick. I've got to find a missing husband who's into a floating poker game—a high-stakes game close by here. Do you know where's it at?"

"Why should I tell you?" Her fleshy pink cheeks wrinkled up.

"You never know when you'll need a favor, girl. You're not exactly a stranger to trouble, Sophie. And I've got this feeling you know where all the action is. So give it up, friend."

"Okay, okay!" She motioned over her shoulder with her

thumb. "It's da little B&B on da *makai* corner—second floor rear. Four knocks'll get you in, but you dint hear it from Sophie, yah?"

"Sure, Sophie." He laid a twenty-dollar bill on the table, knowing full well what the outcome would be, and said, "Cut."

She shuffled the deck and pushed it toward him. He cut and turned over the nine of diamonds. She cut the same deck and turned over the queen of spades. He winked at her.

"See ya, Soph," he said, sliding out of the booth. "Be kind to the suckers, will you?" He grabbed Cane and Able and left the bar.

Sam walked to the cab and parked near the end of a hotel's U-shaped drive. He clipped Goldie's walking leash on, and the two of them strolled to the B&B on the corner. He opened the front door and approached the stairs. Goldie bounded up. Sam climbed, one slow step at a time, clutching the banister.

"Stay," he said softly. Goldie laid herself down on the hall carpet, nose between her paws. Standing on the far side of the door to hide her presence, he knocked sharply four times. The door opened to the chain length and a pair of eyes peered back at him.

"Player," Sam said. The chain slid off, and the door opened fully. Sam stepped inside.

Games were in progress in each of two dimly lit rooms. He took a minute to scan the faces of the men at the tables. None matched the photo Maxine had given him.

"Minimum bet in this room is fifty, two hundred in the back room," said a bruiser in a long-sleeved black shirt. A hotel-style gold name tag said he was called Gardner. "There are no vacancies at any of the tables right now. But you're free to wait over there." With gnarled knuckles, he pointed to a sofa along one wall of the front room, then moved to re-chain the door.

"Wait," said Sam. He pulled Duane and Maxine's picture out of his shirt pocket and showed it to the bouncer. "You seen this guy? He likes to play high-stakes hold-em."

"What the hell do I look like—some kind of nursemaid, brah? Naw. Ain't seen him. Are you a player or not?" The man's narrowed eyes told Sam a different story. He'd recognized the man in the photo.

"I'm a private investigator and I'm looking for a missing husband who's into this game. Take another look," Sam said as he donated a twenty to Duane's cause.

Gardner's belligerent stance eased a bit. He took the bill. "Yeah, he was in here a couple nights ago. A nasty temper, that one. He tapped out about one in the morning and got into it with one of the other players, a regular, mind you. Had the nerve to accuse him of cheating. I threw the troublemaker out on his ear."

"Is the guy he accused in a game here now?" asked Sam.

"How much do you think you can get for one Andy Jackson?" asked Gardner.

"Depends. How much more can you tell me?" Sam fished out his wallet once again, allowing a corner of another twenty to show.

"See the bald guy on the other side of the table? The one with the rich-tourist tan? Only he ain't no tourist."

"Yeah, I see him," said Sam, eyeing the thick gold chain resting on a hairy chest. "Has he got a name?"

"Don't know for sure. I think I heard someone call him Chester, but that may be because of his open shirt. He joins in several times a week wherever the game is played. That's all I can tell you." The bruiser reached for the twenty, snatched it, and slid it into his pants pocket.

Sam nodded and allowed Gardner to unchain the door for him. He stepped out into the hall to find Goldie still lying on the carpet, but busy chewing on something.

"Whatcha got there, girl? Here, let me see." He took a slobbered leather wallet from her mouth and flipped it open. Sure enough, the Ohio driver's license belonged to Duane Fish. The credit cards were gone and so was all the cash. Now he was sure Duane had encountered foul play. "Where, Goldie? Where did you find it?" he whispered.

The dog tilted her head, not knowing what he meant. But

when he held the wallet up she trotted to a window at the opposite end of the hall, where a potted palm stood in a large ceramic tub. She stuck her nose in behind the stalks, then looked back at Sam, snorting to get rid of the dirt flecks. He gave the area the once-over, looking for signs of a struggle, but found none. Satisfied, he wrapped the wallet in his handkerchief and slipped it into one of his cargo-pants pockets. "Let's go, girl," he said as they headed down the stairs to the street. "We're done here."

* * * *

Early Monday morning Sergeant Danny Oshiro received a phone call from Sam. He knew this was no social call when Sam asked him if any unidentified stiffs had turned up in the last few days. Behind wire-rimmed glasses, Danny's keen gray eyes flickered with interest. "We got two John Does, one Asian and one *haole*."

"The *haole*," replied Sam.

"A B&B's kitchen staffer found him in their alley when he was taking out garbage."

Danny's description of the Caucasian—in a blue short-sleeved shirt open at the neck, creased trousers—was close enough that Sam thought he needed to check it out. No need to upset Maxine unless he verified the one John Doe as Duane Fish. Forty-five minutes later, he met Danny at the morgue. A technician pulled the sheet back. Sam held up the anniversary photo, scrutinized it once more, and nodded.

"Yeah, looks like Duane Fish of Cleveland Park, Ohio. He was a tourist and a poker-playing addict. It's the missing person's case I've been working on. I'll bring in the wife later for the formal ID."

"The stiff was worked over pretty good," said Danny, "so he must have pissed off someone along the way." He nodded to the technician, who pulled the sheet down farther.

Sam counted at least ten black-and-blue bruises along the left side of the hairless rib cage.

"There's blunt force trauma on the back of the head as well. What do you know of his earlier whereabouts?" asked Danny.

"He was staying at the Surflyer Hotel with his wife and another couple. He played poker Wednesday and Thursday nights, but didn't come home the second night. The concerned wife hired me on Saturday evening because she hadn't seen him since Thursday. I tracked him down yesterday to the Imperial B&B in Waikīkī. The bouncer said he threw Duane out into the alley around 1:30 a.m. after he went broke and got into a fight. That's the last time anybody claims they saw him alive. By the way, where did you find the poor guy?"

"Lying behind the dumpster in the alley behind the Imperial B&B," Danny said. "He was missing a wallet, a watch, and both shoes. The tox screen said he'd been drinking some, but nowhere close to drunk. The ME says he died between one and three Friday morning, but a full autopsy will be needed to determine the exact time and cause of death."

"You said his wallet, watch, and both shoes were missing? Well, I can account for the wallet anyway." Sam pulled Duane's wallet from his pants pocket, dropped it on an empty morgue steel table, and opened the handkerchief. "Sorry, it's a little slimy. Goldie found it first, but maybe you can get some prints from the inside. Nothing in it but his driver's license. Hey, Danny, how'd you know he was wearing a watch?"

"Simple. He had a tan line on his wrist."

"You figure robbery?"

"It's likely. One scenario might be someone desperate and deprived—maybe a homeless person—with a knowledge of the game upstairs. Could've waited for a well-dressed prospect to come out and rolled him for the watch and shoes."

"One more thing," said Sam. "Was there anything unusual about the crime scene?"

"Not really," said Oshiro. "Your typical hotel back alley with multiple dumpsters and nasty trash. It did stink pretty bad of spoiled fruit juices."

"Thanks, Danny. I guess I'd better inform Maxine Fish of her husband's fate and bring her back for the formal ID."

* * * *

Something about the victim's body nagged at Sam as he drove away from the morgue. It wasn't until he pulled up in front of Auntie Momi's place that it came to him: the bruise marks on Duane's rib cage. They were small and round, too small to be a fist. *What could make such marks?* he wondered.

He rapped on the screen door. "Anybody home?" he yelled.

"Out back, Sam."

He found his auntie and Maxine in the garden, gathering vegetables for supper. Momi was carrying a basket heaped with soil-flecked zucchinis, cherry tomatoes, skinny eggplants, and carrots.

Maxine dispensed with greetings. "Have you found Duane yet?"

"Not exactly," said Sam. "That's why I need your help."

"Whatever do you mean—not exactly?"

"I'll explain on the way. Auntie, she'll be back later. We've got some business to attend to." He led Maxine out to the cab.

Her voice quavered. "Sam, when are you going to explain what you meant back there?"

"Soon, but first I have a couple of questions for you. Did you actually check out of the hotel on Saturday night when I picked you up?"

"No, I just walked away because we had used Duane's credit card when we checked in."

"Do you still have the room's card key with you?"

"Why, yes. I was going to drop it in a mailbox today."

"Good," he said. "Then I'll want to stop by the hotel on our way."

"On our way where?"

"You'll find out shortly," he said. "But first I need to take a look around your hotel room. Will that be okay?"

"Yeah, sure." She lowered her head. Swirls of flaming red hair hardly hid her sullen expression.

Sam parked the cab at one end of the turnaround outside the Surflyer. Leaving Goldie in charge, he and Maxine rode the elevator to the third floor. Maxine unlocked the door and immediately ducked into the bathroom. Sam scanned the room. A half-full bottle of Rémy Martin cognac sat on the glass-topped end table next to the recliner. He tilted it slightly, with the back of his hand, and noted the partial ring it had made underneath.

Satisfied, he shuffled to the closet and pulled open the louvered doors. Inside, he saw a midsized bag and a carry-on, plus the usual polo shirts, aloha shirts, and slacks on hangers. He also found three pairs of men's shoes lined up on the floor: sandals, loafers, and leather dress shoes. He picked up each of the shoes, one by one, sniffed it, then laid the sandals and loafers back on the floor. Hastily, he unzipped the carry-on, which was empty, dropped the black dress shoes inside, then zipped it back up. He had shut the closet door and was ready to leave when Maxine came out of the bathroom.

"Find what you were looking for?" she asked.

"If you don't mind, I'm borrowing your husband's carry-on," he told her as he rolled it out to the hall.

"I don't understand why, but I guess it's okay. Damn, you're one mysterious guy," she said as they rode the elevator down to the lobby.

Sam punched in Danny's number. "Yo, Danny. Sam here. Next stop 835 Iwilei Road. Be there in twenty minutes."

"Copy that," said Oshiro.

"What's that address?" Maxine asked.

"It belongs to the police," said Sam evasively.

* * * *

The uniformed receptionist informed them that Sergeant Oshiro had not arrived yet, but they could take a seat in an adjacent waiting room.

"Is this place a morgue?" Maxine asked, a tremor in her voice. She had put two and two together and come up with the obvious answer. "Is Duane—?

76

"I think so," Sam replied as he studied her face. "I didn't tell you earlier so you wouldn't get upset in advance. I'm not absolutely positive. I don't want you to get upset now, but the police have discovered a body that may fit Duane's description. If it is him, your identification may prove invaluable to them and, of course, you. I'll be there for you if you want me. We're waiting for the detective in charge of this case."

Danny arrived ten minutes later, and the three of them were ushered into a viewing room. When they were in position, Danny spoke into a microphone. "We're ready." A curtain drew back on the other side of a window, revealing a gurney with a covered body.

Oshiro turned to Maxine. "Are you ready, ma'am?" he asked gently. She nodded, her face free of makeup, chalky with anxiety. "Okay," Oshiro called out. The sheet was peeled back just to chest level, so that a less gruesome picture might be presented.

Maxine, who had turned away, now inched back around to confront the truth. She bit her lip. "Yes, that's Duane," she said, her voice trembling. "Enough!" In tears she reeled away, and the curtain was closed.

When the trio returned to the waiting room and were sitting again, Sam turned to Maxine. "Mrs. Fish, why did you kill your husband?"

"What did you say?" Her voice cracked.

"You heard me. I began to suspect you when I saw the tiny bruise marks all over the left side of your husband's rib cage. They were made by a woman's stiletto heel—like the kind you're wearing now," he said. "A woman acting out a powerful vengeance. You followed him to the poker game Thursday night and waited for him to come out."

"But he didn't!" Maxine blurted out. "I'd been waiting on a bench in front for, like, three hours and then I heard a commotion out back behind the B&B, so I ducked around the back and saw my loser of a husband being tossed out the door and into the alley. He was stumbling but still on his feet."

"That sounds about right," Sam said. "You must've been mad as hell, so you went along with your plan. You hit him on the back of the head."

"I didn't hit him that hard," she said, changing her tone to a staged whimper. "But I was furious. I shoved him across the alley behind the dumpster. It was overflowing and he fell down into a pile of garbage—sickening, rotting restaurant food and an empty carton from POG sloshing all over the ground. He looked so disgusting, and then he fell on his face with his pants and shoes getting all wet from the POG crap. So I just walked away and caught a cab back to the hotel."

"Don't lie to us, Maxine," Sam said. "Maybe you hit him harder than you intended to. But then you turned him over on his back and finished the job by kicking him in the ribs repeatedly and mercilessly, venting anger you couldn't control."

Maxine shot back, "So I kicked him a few times. It doesn't mean I killed him. Why pick on me? There are lots of people out there who could've done it."

But Sam was prepared. "Oh, but I think you did. The ME said Duane died of blunt-force trauma. I'm guessing you used the bottle of Rémy Martin cognac as a weapon. I saw it in your room and the sticky, bloody ring it made on the end table. You should have been more careful when you wiped the bottle clean. You prob'ly hid it in that big fancy purse of yours when you followed him. If you hadn't meant to kill him, why would you have taken it along?"

Her face contorted with anger. "You meddling bastard. I should've known better than to hire you. I paid a hundred bucks for that bottle. I want it back!"

Sam's dark eyes burned into hers. "Aha! So that's why you carried it back to the room and foolishly left it behind. Sorry, Maxine, Forensics has it. It's the murder weapon and evidence now." Calmly, he continued, pointing his index finger straight at her.

"Then I began to think. The police found him without his shoes. Why would the killer take off your husband's dress shoes?

78

HIGH STAKES IN HONOLULU

There's one obvious answer. You planned to blame a homeless person, a ruse to throw the police off. I needed to see Duane's luggage and stuff in your room. Sure enough! You, Mrs. Fish, provided that opportunity—allowing me access to your hotel room. When you were in the bathroom, I found sandals, loafers, and dress shoes in the closet. Sergeant Oshiro told me about the mess at the crime scene, the overflowing dumpster. So I decided to smell all the shoes in the closet. The dress shoes, especially the laces, reeked of rancid pineapple, orange, and guava juices, as I suspected. Those shoes are in my trunk, packed in your husband's carry-on bag. I'm sure the lab technicians will link them to the crime scene, and if you left any prints, they'll link them to you as well."

"That was an illegal search!" Maxine shouted. She leaped up from the vinyl chair, stomped her elegant Gucci pump, then twisted her hips to slide her body in front of her Prada hobo bag.

"No way," said Sam. "I accompanied you to the room, and you willingly opened the door for me. I asked you if I could look around, and you said yes. You cooperated with my search. And don't forget, you hired me to act on your behalf. There's only one way the shoes got from the crime scene to your hotel room. You took them there to hide them in plain sight. You thought it would be a sure-fire way to deflect suspicion from yourself onto an innocent homeless person."

Maxine lunged forward, looking toward the double doors to escape. She was counting on out-muscling Danny, but he was already on his feet. Her constricting skin-tight silk pants and spike heels were no match for Danny's martial arts skills. His one karate kick threw her off her feet. She shrieked and tumbled to the floor. Pulling her up by one arm, he shoved her against the wall and clamped cuffs on her wrists behind her back. While reciting her Miranda rights, he led her out through those same doors.

Sam followed. Settling into the cab, he chatted with his partner. "Let's go home, girl. We still have our thousand-dollar fee—for two days' work. A whole lot more than we'd make for our taxi services. But we got our man—or rather, woman. Didn't we,

Detective Goldie?"

    Still thinking aloud, he said, "Death by cognac. Now there's a sobering thought."

    "Rrruff!"

§

Episode Six
Tripped Up

PEGGY AND HER DAD SAT ON A PARK BENCH UNDER A cluster of monkeypod trees not too far from the western edge of Ala Moana (meaning "Path to the Sea") Beach Park. Sam was scooping out pistachio ice cream from a cardboard cup with a wooden spoon. Peggy lifted up the last two inches of her Rocky Road cone in Goldie's direction. A long pink tongue arrived before the rest of her, and any trace of ice cream soon became a memory. It was one of those glorious Sundays father and daughter got to spend together—a matinee movie, late afternoon in the park, and supper.

Sam collected their trash, rolled it into a ball, and flipped it into the nearby rubbish container with a high-arcing basketball shot. "A three-pointer if I ever saw one," he said. "Hey, Peggs, have I told you about Goldie's newest trick for bringing down bad guys?"

"Uh-uh. Is it dangerous for her or only the bad guys?"

Sam squinted as he thought about it, creased lines emanating from the outside corners of his eyes. "Could be both, I suppose, but I would use it only in emergencies. After all, I do run a Private Eye business, dear. We've gotten into some pretty hairy situations."

"So how does it work, the trick?"

"Well, if I open and close my left fist a few times, Goldie

81

will circle around behind the culprit, run at them, and throw her whole body squarely at the back of their knees and knock them over. If anybody gets the drop on me with a handgun, it could save my life."

"I'd like to see Goldie do it. Try it out on me, Daddy."

"No, it's too rough. You'd get hurt and I'd never forgive myself."

"Pleeeeease! The grass is plenty thick over there. Besides, I've got jeans on. And I promise I won't tell Mom."

Sam's black eyebrows arched as he shook his head in dismay. "Peggs, I know you say you won't tell Mom, but it would slip out anyhow because you'd consider it a big adventure. Young lady, we do not keep secrets from your mother. And do you know what would happen if I did let you be my guinea pig? Mom would march right down to the courthouse and revoke my visiting rights. And I wouldn't blame her. So the answer is, Absolutely not."

Goldie knew they were talking about her. Sensing Peggy's sulking displeasure, she nuzzled against her favorite kid's leg.

Peggy knelt down and tickled Goldie behind both ears. "I'm fine, old girl. That's quite a trick you learned."

"Now I suppose you're angry with me for being so protective," said her father.

"Yeah," she said, faking a pout. "But I do get it, Daddy. Can we go for supper anyway?" She jumped up and laid her head against her father's shoulder. "How about Big City Diner?"

"Sure thing. Just what I had in mind."

The trio slowly made their way across the grass and the white stone pedestrian bridge to Ala Moana Boulevard at the Queen Street crossing. The light changed favorably and they walked a short block to Auahi Street and crossed over to the other side. They were heading toward Kamakeʻe Street and the diner in the Ward Entertainment Center, where Sam had parked his cab. The half-hour walk was taking a little more out of him than he was used to. He was getting stronger by the day, but still…Leaning with his full weight on his canes, he felt the pressure and soreness in his shoulders, forearms, and wrists. His hands definitely felt less sore now that he'd discovered weightlifters' gloves for cushioning.

They were just passing "Hello Gorgeous," a new boutique on Auahi, when a burglar alarm went off. They heard a ruckus inside and someone shouting, "Stop, thief!" A tall female in a purple top and cut-off jeans ran out of the store and crashed into Sam from his right side, knocking him off his canes. He landed butt-first on the concrete sidewalk.

Without so much as a hasty apology, the woman darted away and disappeared among strolling shoppers.

Angry and bruised, Sam assumed the fleeing woman was the thief. He gave Goldie her new fist signal. The retriever took off after her. A half-block ahead, Goldie caught up within three feet of her, lunged forward, and slammed into the back of her knees, throwing her forward to the ground. The woman's large shoulder bag went flying. It fell with a thud and flipped open on the pavement, scattering a few of the contents. Goldie clamped her jaws about the culprit's bare right ankle, intending to keep her grounded until Sam arrived. That is, until a stranger interfered.

A Good Samaritan pedestrian stepped forward. Fortyish, wearing a Reyn Spooner designer shirt and khakis, he hovered over Goldie and scolded her while clapping his hands and stomping his feet. "Go away! Scat!"

Confused and intimidated by this stranger and the mixed signals, Goldie released her grip on the ankle and backed off.

The man knelt to help the woman collect her spilled possessions: a compact, lipstick, comb, a thin wallet, and the weighty shoulder bag itself. With a mumbled ungracious "Thanks," she threw it all back into her bag, jumped up, and disappeared into the curious gathering crowd.

This drama played out just seconds before Sam and Peggy caught up. Goldie made whimpering sounds to cover her doggie guilt. Somehow she felt she had displeased her master.

Seeing Sam bend to check out and reassure Goldie, the do-gooder laced into him. "Is that your nasty dog, mister? You ought

83

to be ashamed, letting him run loose without a leash. He attacked a woman only a few minutes ago right here on the sidewalk. I had to chase him off and help the lady to her feet. It was the gentlemanly thing to do. I—"

"First of all, Mister Buttinsky," interrupted Peggy, hands on her hips. "My father's dog is a she. Second, both my father and Goldie here are trained to catch criminals. He's a private investigator. And third, the woman you just made nice with robbed a store back there. And during her escape, she knocked my father off his canes—he's disabled. So thanks to your interference she made a clean getaway."

The do-gooder looked stricken. A merciless scolding from a kid.

"Enough, Peggy!" said Sam, shocked and embarrassed by his daughter's brazen behavior, but also reluctantly impressed by her well-organized mind as she lectured this stranger. "The gentleman had no way of knowing. He was only trying to do the right thing. Furthermore, the woman is the *alleged* thief. We have no proof yet."

Goldie had recovered her normal confidence. She was busy sniffing at a sheet of paper lying on the sidewalk.

"Whatcha got there, girl?" Sam asked. Goldie managed to pick up the tri-folded paper between her teeth and deliver it to him with a minimum of drool.

"Well, this is interesting. It's a Hawai'ian Electric Company bill."

"It probably came from *her* purse," said the subdued do-gooder, whose clean-shaven face was now pale. "Some stuff fell out when she went down on her face. I helped her pick it all up."

"Electric bills have names and addresses, isn't that so, Daddy?" Peggy asked.

"Of course, sweetie," he replied, reading the name Carly Adams. "Plus an account number. We've hit the jackpot. Oh boy—there's a 'Past Due, Third Warning' notice at the bottom." Sam carefully slid the bill into one of his deep cargo pants pockets.

84

The still-lingering Good Samaritan, eager to make amends, said, "Sounds like a desperate person turning to thievery."

"Sir? I just realized I don't know your name," said Sam.

"Mortimer Franks." He fumbled through his pockets and handed Sam a business card, complete with email and phone number.

"Mr. Franks, I'm a—" started Sam.

"Call me Mort. It's less formal."

"Mort, I'm a licensed private investigator." Sam held out his credentials. "My daughter only got a side and rear view of the alleged perpetrator. The woman crashed into me as she was running out the door, so I saw zilch, being sprawled out on my 'ōkole on the sidewalk." Sam smiled wryly. "I'm hoping you got a good look at her. Could you pick her out of a crowd, by any chance?"

"You better believe it," said Mort. "Maybe late twenties, early thirties. Real pretty blonde hair, kind of long. Curls spilling out all over the place and tortoise-shell glasses. Sleeveless top. Oh yeah—a goose tattoo on her left shoulder. Know what I mean?"

"A nēnē, the Hawai'ian goose? Black head, gray-brown?"

"Yeah."

"Great! Thank you, Mort," said Sam. "That's an excellent description."

Mort's eyes shifted to the ground with embarrassment. "Uh, yeah. For a second there I was actually thinking of asking her out for a cup of coffee. But…I guess I'm not a very good judge of character."

"You're a good man, Mort," said Sam. "No way you could've known. I'll be reporting your description to the police right away, so you'll be hearing from them shortly."

"Glad to help." Mort Franks nodded to them and walked off.

"Sweetheart, we have to wait with dinner until I put in a call to the police. Okay?"

"Sure, Daddy," Peggy said, her eyes bright and face flushed from all the excitement. "What's another five minutes?" She tied her sweat jacket sleeves around her waist.

Sam pulled out his cell and punched in HPD headquarters. "Robbery Division please…Sam Nahoe. I believe I have some good intel on a robbery on Auahi about half an hour ago.…The shop owner called it in? Good. Who caught the case?…Pop Lione? You think he's at the scene now?…Thanks, I'm only a block away. I'll touch base with him." Sam hung up and turned to Peggy. "Well, hon, it's gonna be more than five minutes. I can drop you off at home, or you can tag along while I go back to the scene of the crime and give them our information."

Peggy bounced up and down in her sneakers, barely containing herself. "Are you kidding, Daddy? I'm staying with you. This is so thrilling. I've never been to a crime scene before."

The Hello Gorgeous boutique had dazzling window displays on both sides of the glass doors: patterned silk tops and minidresses for the sophisticated female. They found a uniformed cop stretching yellow crime scene tape across the front of the shop, and a cruiser with flashing blue lights sitting curbside.

Sam approached and flashed his PI credentials. "Aloha. Would you inform Sergeant Lione that Sam Nahoe has some information for him and would like to talk with him? It's important."

The uniform disappeared inside and a few minutes later reappeared with his sergeant, who was wearing Latex gloves and cloth footies. Pop wasn't as old as his nickname sounded. He was prematurely gray, but had a round, young face and darting eyes. "Hey, Sam, got a hot one here. Can't be socializing."

"Here I came to solve your case for you, and you can't take any time for me?"

"What's this solve-my-case-for-me business?" asked Pop.

"My daughter, Peggy, and myself, and Goldie here were passing this shop when the robbery took place." Sam continued with a precise report, including Mort's description. "The perp ran out and knocked me on my *'ōkole*. I was so angry, I sicced Goldie on her, and she ran the woman down about a half-block west of here. Goldie would have held her until I got there, except some bystander interfered, and she got away. This is the guy's business card. Mortimer Franks. Said he could pick her out of a lineup. Give him a call."

"Daddy, don't forget the electric bill."

"Right you are, Peggs." Sam carefully lifted it out of his pocket and held it out to Pop.

"What's this?" asked Pop.

"The woman's purse spilled open when Goldie brought her down. Franks even helped her pick up her stuff, but they both missed this: a HECO bill. My dog found it lying on the sidewalk. So there you have it." Sam grinned at his former colleague. "So, Pop, case all wrapped up?"

"Maybe," said Pop. "Thanks for the assist. I'll call it in, contact Mr. Franks, and send a car around to locate the woman."

"By the way, Pop, how much did she get away with?"

"She made the proprietor clean out the register for about eight hundred dollars. Not much by most robbery standards, but the woman did brandish a gun, and that's armed robbery."

"No kidding?" Sam turned to Peggy. "Well, dear, our job here is done. Let's get that dinner."

When they arrived at the entrance to the Big City Diner, they asked to be seated.

The host responded, "Sorry, sir, no dogs inside."

Sam looked around and saw half a dozen wrought-iron tables on the lanai just outside the door. "Do you serve food at these tables?"

"Mainly drinks, but sure do. Help yourself to one of them."

"Looks like we're gonna have dinner under the stars," said Peggy. "Cool!"

Dusk had fallen, and a few stars had managed to expose themselves, despite the nearby neon haze. Sam settled for a small round table near the railing, perfect for the loose end of Goldie's leash. A motherly local waitress came to take their orders. She brought two glasses of water and an apron pocketful of silverware and napkins.

"Hi, I'm Polina," she said. "What can I get you?"

"I want the ahi salad and fries and a Diet Coke," said Peggy, looking at her dad for approval.

He nodded. "And I'll have the full rack of baby-back ribs, baked potato, and coleslaw. And a hamburger on rice, no gravy, on a paper plate for my lady friend down here." He patted Goldie on the head. "A bowl of water for her would be nice too."

"She's a beaut," offered the smiling waitress while she scribbled on her order pad. "You want the works on that baked potato?"

"Of course." Sam beamed with a impish grin.

Peggy knew better than to criticize what her father chose to eat. His physical limitations had made her more sensitive to him. Instead, she gazed around the Ward complex and surrounding congestion. "We used to be able to see the park from here," she said. "Now it's just one high-rise after another. They're destroying Honolulu's natural beauty."

"I agree," said Sam. "The developers and politicians seem to be in cahoots. Maybe your generation can do better than mine."

"By then it'll be too late. Oh, here comes our food."

Polina set her tray down on an adjacent table and brought their tabletop dinners first. Then she set Goldie's order on the floor. Goldie nosed into her food with a vengeance, but the paper plate kept sliding away on the polished concrete until she stepped onto the plate with a front paw. She inhaled her dinner, then looked up at Sam with her pleading eyes. Sam took one look at the accomplished beggar and steeled himself. The vet had warned him that large dogs, especially overweight ones, were susceptible to hip injuries.

"No, Goldie, lie down!"

She meekly obeyed.

They munched on their meals as Polina served a patron at a nearby table. Goldie, on the other hand, was always alert to her surroundings, especially now that she had finished her meager supper. Rising, she pulled to the limits of her leash and tried to sniff at a lately arrived female patron, but the air was so full of distracting pungent food aromas that she was unsure. While she strained at the end of her leash, an offshore breeze cleared her nasal passage. She began to growl.

"What's wrong with Goldie?" asked Peggy. "That's not like her at all. She's looking at the woman at that table."

"And acting like she recognizes her. But it can't be Carly Adams. That woman has short brown hair," said Sam. "Not curly blonde. She *is* wearing tortoise-shell glasses, though. Hey! There's a tattoo on her left shoulder and, by God, it's a *nēnē!*"

"Oh-oh, now she's looking straight at us," whispered Peggy. "The blonde hair must've been a wig, and she must've ditched that big bag she had."

They heard a loud scraping sound as the woman pushed back the wrought iron chair across the concrete and stood. Obviously recognizing Goldie, she mouthed the words "Damn it" and backed away from her table. Carly's right hand dug deep into an open black purse and stayed there. Sam grabbed Cane and Able, stood up, and took a few steps in her direction.

"Stop right there, Buster, and don't interfere!"

Sam jerked to a halt. Carly's right hand now held a revolver pointed straight at him. Cold sweat formed in his armpits. His back spasmed with fear for his daughter. "Peggy!" he whispered. "Go inside and call 9-1-1." To Carly, he said, "You don't really want to shoot anybody now, do you?"

"No," she retorted, her blue eyes cloudy with anger. "I don't want to shoot you, but I will. So butt out, mister. You too, girl. Go back to your table and sit down! Or else!"

Sam reasoned that Carly had three escape choices. One, the ground-level parking in the garage, where she could escape through an exit at the other end. Two, make a mad dash toward the street and run. Or three, take the elevator up to the movie theater level. Choices one and two meant she'd have to take her chances with Goldie chasing her again. As Sam expected, Carly

89

chose the theater level, which offered the most escape routes—too many and too difficult for even him to follow. Still clutching the revolver, Carly darted into the lobby and pressed the elevator button. What she didn't count on was the elevator arriving packed full of theater patrons, leaving after the end of a movie. She stood facing the open door with the gun prominent, her legs planted wide in defiance. The elevator walls reverberated with frantic multiple screams. Someone inside was resourceful enough to re-close the doors and send the elevator back up to the theater floor. Carly had no chance to make a move. In truth, she had no plan at all.

Peggy either had not heard her father's command to go inside the restaurant or chose not to. She had totally fixated on the dog. She didn't know whether she could get Goldie to do her new trick or not, but it was worth a try. She unclipped the leash, then opened and closed her left fist three times.

Still facing the elevator, Carly didn't see the flash of russet-gold fur approaching behind her. Goldie slammed into the young woman's knees, taking her to the floor and dislodging the gun from her grip. It slid several yards out of her reach as she lay sprawled out on her stomach.

Goldie placed her front paws and then her full weight on Carly's back. Within seconds, Sam arrived and removed a tie-wrap restraint from his belt pouch, a man-purse of sorts, and bound the woman's hands behind her back. Clapping his own hands sharply, he gave Goldie the release signal. She backed off. Sam's clapping also initiated unsolicited applause from the gathering of frightened but curious onlookers. Goldie thanked them with a short bark. She hadn't been taught to bow—yet.

With a gloved hand, Sam picked up the revolver, a Saturday night special. All the chambers were empty! The gun had been unloaded all this time. Carly couldn't have shot anyone.

Peggy had belatedly responded to her father's command and called 9-1-1 on her smart phone. A cruiser arrived promptly with Pop Lione and another uniformed officer on board. Pop read the pathetic perpetrator her Miranda rights.

When father and daughter finally sat down again to finish their food, Peggy brought up a troubling thought. "Daddy, if Carly's gun wasn't loaded, does she still have to go to jail for a long time?"

"Yes," he said. "Just brandishing a gun, even an empty one, posed a terroristic threat, even if she hadn't received any money as a result."

"What will happen to her?"

"The young woman will probably plead guilty and be sentenced to three to five years for armed robbery."

It was time to take Peggy home to her mom. Before heading to their cab, she wrapped her arms around her father's waist and looked up at him. "Daddy? Thank you for protecting me from that awful woman—and for not testing out Goldie's new trick on me." Her chocolate-brown eyes took on a mischievous twinkle. "Besides, Daddy, Goldie wouldn't have obeyed you."

Sam grinned and hugged her back. "You got that right, sweetie."

A week later an envelope arrived from the Hello Gorgeous boutique. The proprietor, grateful to the whole Nahoe family, including Goldie, gave Peggy a $200 gift certificate. There was even an article in the *Honolulu Star-Advertiser,* but at Sam's request, only Goldie's name was mentioned.

Episode Seven
The Kidnapped Youngster

THE LITTLE BOY'S CHORTLING LAUGH ROUSED SAM FROM A snooze on the park bench. He looked up and saw a young Asian woman sitting on a bench not twenty feet away. She seemed to be dividing her attention between her smart phone and her kid playing with his toy truck. He casually smiled at her. She stared back at him with a cold, blank look.

At age thirty-eight Sam noticed that he usually still turned women's heads, and was surprised when he didn't. At this moment he wondered, *What the devil? Does she think I'm trying to pick her up? I guess she doesn't see my two canes.*

He'd gotten accustomed to his four parallel lives: cab driver; private investigator with zero clients right now; divorced dad with only visiting rights; and the worst of it, disabled ex-detective. Even as a licensed independent cabbie, Sam wasn't privy to taxi stands or a formal dispatcher. He relied on fares he could pick up while cruising, or from repeat and word-of-mouth business. At slow times he had to park somewhere to save on gas. On this too-quiet Thursday afternoon in June, he chose Magic Island, actually a small peninsula jutting out into the Pacific Ocean from Ala Moana Beach Park. Of course, he left his business cell phone on all the time.

Sam felt a tug on the leash. He had trained Goldie well

as his clever, responsive partner. But she'd always be a playful dog at heart and couldn't resist looking for someone or something to frolic with. Trotting from her longish leash to within a few feet of the youngster, she sat down to watch him. Sam glanced over at the handsome boy with rounded head of black hair and fair complexion. The child had already tired of his truck and traded it for a soccer ball out of his mother's tote bag. He kicked it toward Goldie. She batted it with her nose all the way back to him. Sam watched keenly. Giggling, the agile boy kicked the ball a few feet farther. Goldie joyfully responded again. The next time, the child gave it a mighty boot and chased the ball himself beyond Goldie's reach. A slight incline in the terrain sent it rolling faster and farther away. Goldie uttered a shrill bark. The mother looked up from her iPhone—texting, game-playing, or whatever was preoccupying her. But by that time, both boy and ball had traveled at least fifty yards in the direction of the parking lot.

She sprang up and yelled, "Paulie, come back here this instant! Let the ball go!"

Either ignoring or not hearing his mother, the boy charged gleefully on.

Sam hefted himself up off the bench, yanked the leash close, and unclipped it. "Fetch him, Goldie! Go!" Relying on his canes, despite the stabbing pain in his lower back, he managed to get down the incline, quite near. But before his dog could reach the child, Sam witnessed a horrific sight.

A large man in a T-shirt and khaki shorts stepped out from behind a monkeypod tree, grabbed Paulie around the waist with gloved hands, and lifted him up.

Paulie, wiggling, struggling, legs flailing, shrieked "Mommy!" The man hauled him off into a gray pickup truck parked in the lot next to the grass and slammed the passenger door shut.

Barking all the way, Goldie closed in, but the man had already climbed into the truck and turned on the ignition. The pickup began rolling past the aisles of cars toward the exit. Goldie was prepared to give chase, but a sharp whistle from Sam brought

93

her back. He knew she wouldn't be able to keep up, and a chase through the parking lot would only put her in danger from cars arriving or leaving. He managed to catch a partial plate number just before the pickup turned right, passed the lineup of outrigger canoes awaiting the high-school paddlers, and headed out to Ala Moana Boulevard.

Screaming, clutching her phone, tote, and purse, Paulie's mother ran to the edge of the parking lot and stopped short. Frantic and forlorn, she knew her precious child had been kidnapped.

Sam realized the grotesque irony of the scene. If it had been a weekend, Magic Island would have been teeming with locals: on all-day picnics; fishermen wading as they cast their lines; surfers carrying their boards; brides and grooms posing for photographers. Half the Honolulu world at play. The kidnapper would never have made it out of the park. In fact, he'd probably never have even found a parking space.

Sam speed-dialed 9-1-1 and gave the HPD dispatcher what little he'd observed. A tall, thickset Caucasian in tan T-shirt and shorts. Long hair tied in a ponytail. Gun-metal gray Toyota pickup, older model, and the partial plate. After he rattled off his own credentials, former badge number, and his Checker Cab plates, he was promised that an alert would be issued shortly.

He signed off and turned to the child's mother, who was pacing back and forth. "Ma'am, I phoned the police dispatcher. A cruiser will be here any minute."

"That horrible man took my baby! Why Paulie? Why him?" Tears streaked down her pale, gaunt cheeks, outlined by black automatic hair that draped her bony shoulders. She wore an embroidered aqua blouse and matching Capri pants.

A designer getup, Sam decided. "Ma'am, I'm a former HPD detective, a private investigator now," he said, extending his credentials so she could see them. "While we're waiting for the police, may I ask you a few questions?"

Still eyeing him suspiciously, she said, "Okay, but why aren't they here yet? He's getting away with my Paulie."

"Can you tell me your name?"

"Cynthia Set Fong. My husband is Douglas Ang Fong. He's a well-known lawyer here."

Sam recognized the name: a big-time defense attorney.

"And the boy's full name, please."

"Paul Ang Fong. He just turned four."

"Did you recognize either the man who took your son or the truck he drove?" asked Sam.

"No, why would I?" Her voice had an imperious ring to it.

"Could he have been a family member?"

"No member of our family would do such a thing," she retorted.

"Or could it be a known enemy of your husband?"

"I have no way of knowing that," she snapped, her head lowered as she speed-dialed her husband with manicured nails. "He's with a client?" Cynthia asked shrilly. "This is an extreme emergency. Disturb him anyway!"

The police cruiser pulled up in front of them. Missing Persons Detective Mitchell Bailey, mustached and squarely built, exchanged curt greetings with Sam and took down all his information. Sam and Mitch had known each other briefly at HPD. Slightly annoyed, Mitch thought Sam should have waited for him to arrive and ask the questions, but conceded that time was critical and Sam was, after all, a PI now.

He introduced himself to Mrs. Fong. "Ma'am, what is your son wearing?"

Her troubled eyes peered over his left shoulder, hoping against hope that Paulie would magically reappear. "A red and white checked shirt and jeans. White and black sneakers."

"Do you have a photo of him, Mrs. Fong?"

Cynthia opened her smart phone once again, and swiped to the photo, then extended it taller with thumb and forefinger. "This is Paulie at his fourth birthday party last month." Sam looked over Bailey's shoulder and studied the photo. It showed a boy with an impish, happy grin and one front tooth missing. Feet planted apart, he stood arms raised with fists clenched and mock biceps in a white martial arts outfit. Almost apologetically, Mom said, "His bangs are lopsided, he was so squirmy in the barber chair. His grandmother bought him the suit. He just loves the dragon."

"Excellent, Mrs. Fong." Mitch recited the HPD email address for Cynthia to immediately relay the photo to Missing Persons.

The frightened mother, barely controlled up to now, grew more and more agitated, and stamped her sandaled foot. "Why aren't you out there looking for my son?"

"That's exactly what we're about to do, Mrs. Fong," said Mitch. "Now that we have your son's photo and other information, HPD will now issue a MAILE AMBER ALERT."

"What is that?" she demanded.

"It stands for Minor Abducted in Life-threatening Emergency." He refrained from the grisly details: that MAILE and AMBER were named in memory of two abducted, murdered little girls. "All HPD officers will be out there doing everything in their power to find your son. I still need a little more information from you."

Sam signaled Mitch with a complimentary half-salute that he was leaving. "Come on, Goldie, I don't think we're needed here any longer," he said, heading for their cab a few aisles away. He hooked Goldie into her harness and drove off, passing the police car with another wave. He pondered the ugly situation. *Is this a random kidnapping to acquire a child or a targeted one to extract a ransom? Does it have something to do with the husband? Maybe revenge by a former client he didn't succeed in getting off—like a convicted felon now out on parole?*

* * * *

Early the next afternoon, Sam had just dropped off a customer on King Street when he got a call from the detective asking him to stop by an address on Kapi'olani Boulevard. When he and Goldie arrived, Mitch and FBI Agent Will Manning were waiting for him. He rolled down the window.

Sam had never met Manning, who wore the typical agent's

dark suit and white shirt, but open at the neck. No tie, maybe because of the eighty-five-degree day, but more likely, the sweaty frustration of yet one more child-abduction case. Manning looked grim.

"Last night the Fongs received a call on their landline, voice disguised, demanding a ransom of $200,000 in the boy's bookbag. We were with them and tried to trace the call, but it was from a burner phone. Just ten minutes ago, Cynthia got a call on her cell. The same disguised voice instructed her to order a taxi to pick her up—only her with the ransom money—outside their high-rise on Kapiʻolani at exactly 2:15. She's supposed to receive further instructions to give the driver once they're under way. Douglas Fong withdrew the ransom money from their bank this morning in accordance with the untraceable call they'd received the night before."

"Two-fifteen? That's only twenty minutes from now," said Sam. "How the devil are you going to work that one?"

"That's exactly why I thought of you, Sam," said Mitch. "You're already familiar with the case and the neighborhoods on Oʻahu. We don't have time to set up anything else. The apartment is in the next block. When you pull up to the building, Mrs. Fong will come out carrying the bookbag with the money and get into your cab. We don't know if they're watching the building or not, so we have to play it close to the vest. I should ask, Are you willing to handle this?"

"Of course. I feel for those parents, and Paulie Fong is a cute little guy, but that's beside the point. We need to find him before he's harmed. My partner and I will do whatever it takes."

Agent Manning stared at Goldie. He frowned. "That's your partner?"

"You bet," said Sam.

Manning shrugged. "Okay, then." He checked his watch. "Wait ten minutes, then pull into the semicircular drive out front. Oh, I almost forgot. Dial this number, keep your cell phone open, and repeat your instructions out loud. She was told 'No police.'

We'll follow at a safe distance."

Sam set up the phone on the dashboard, lingered the ten minutes, and took off down the block. He pulled into the drive, stopped at the entrance, and waited. A minute or two later, Cynthia Fong, in a navy-blue pants outfit, emerged from the lobby of the upscale condo, and climbed into the back seat carrying her son's black bookbag with its Puma logo. Her face reflected a mix of fear and determination. The dark circles under her eyes told Sam she'd probably been up all night. He waited until he heard her cell ring tone.

"Yesss," she answered, her voice trembling, and then began to repeat aloud. "Head east on Kapiʻolani to the freeway entrance and get on H-1 East." A little under five minutes later, she parroted, "Get off the freeway at the Sixth Avenue exit. On the ramp turn left onto Sixth Avenue and move to the far right lane. Pull into the Eden Presbyterian Church driveway in the middle of the block just before Harding." She paused and added, to Sam: "Then I'm supposed to get out."

Sam followed the instructions until he realized he wouldn't be able to hear Cynthia once she had left the cab. He pulled into the driveway and braked. She slid out with the bookbag clutched in her left hand, and her right hand gluing the phone to her ear. Walking shakily back to the avenue, she turned left toward the highway overpass. In a flash Sam knew what the kidnapper had in mind. *She's been told to drop the money bag off the overpass onto the service lane on the freeway.* But in which direction?

Sam reacted quickly. He drove up the church driveway to the empty parking lot and U-turned. Inching back toward Sixth Avenue, he watched Cynthia stop at the near edge of the overpass and lean over. *Westbound! That means it will take at least sixty seconds for the kidnapper to retrieve the drop and get back in his car. Is that enough time for me to go around the block to the H-1 West entrance? I'll try!*

Sam turned right on Sixth, then left on Harding against the light between two horn-blowing cars headed in opposite directions, and left again at the Fifth Avenue ramp onto the freeway. On the ramp two cars ahead of him, he discovered a silver Honda sedan accelerating away from the westbound service lane. He'd found his quarry. The perp had been too smart to keep using his pickup truck.

Sam accelerated to fall in behind the Honda with only one car between them. As soon as he got into position he spoke to his open cell phone, explaining that he was on the freeway following the money car. The silver Honda slowed and turned onto the University Avenue ramp. Sam relayed the "turns" instructions and followed. They passed the UH campus and headed north into Mānoa Valley, then onto Mānoa Road, deeper into the thickly wooded neighborhoods with narrow streets. A few turns later, the Honda slowed and swerved into the driveway of a single-story bungalow. Sam drove past it, did a U-turn at the next intersection, and parked a few doors down on the opposite side of the street to watch. The Honda driver—the burly scumbag who had abducted Paulie—got out of the car with the bookbag and carried it around to the rear of the house.

Damn! Paulie isn't in the car, concluded Sam. He reported the house address to Mitch, who told him to stay in the cab.

"By the way," said Sam, as he rolled all his windows down and turned off the ignition. "Could you send someone to pick up Mrs. Fong? I left her at the overpass. She must be busting a gut and spitting mad by now."

"We're way ahead of you, Sam," said Mitch. "Her husband went to pick her up as soon as you left her. She must be with him already. We'll be with you in five or six minutes."

Sam saw a light come on in the front room of the house. He unhooked his partner's harness. "Stay," he ordered. "Stay, Goldie!" He scanned the property, assessing how close he could get without being seen. In the front yard he would get help from a low-branched plumeria tree, lavishly in bloom with clusters of white blossoms. He grabbed Cane and Able, climbed slowly out of the cab, and plodded across the street. Approaching the small house from the side, he tried to get a better look, maybe even inside. The front windows were a little high, but he noticed the driveway grade increased some toward the back, so he inched along between the house and the parked Honda. At first, all he could see was a dark form inside, but now another light came on, and he saw two male adults moving about.

There was no sign of the boy, so Sam ski-walked to a second window, but stumbled and kicked an empty soda can on its side. It rolled noisily down the asphalt driveway. Expecting a threat from the back of the house, he ducked behind the Honda, keeping it between him and the house. Crouched down and quiet, he was jolted by a raspy male voice behind him.

"Get up and reach for the sky, snoop."

Sam awkwardly stood, raising his hands and canes in the air. He tried to turn and face the voice, but a shove in the shoulder told him "Forget it!"

Sam caught a glimpse of a gun pointed at his neck, but took the offensive anyway. "Hey, scumbag, where's the boy?"

"I'll ask the questions. Who the hell are you and what are you doing here?"

Before Sam could answer, a huge bundle of fur slammed into the man's side, taking him off his feet onto his back. Sam was actually startled. Goldie had jumped out the passenger side window, against his command to stay. But he couldn't have been more relieved. The gun had fallen onto the driveway. He now got a good look at his assailant. Yup, it was the kidnapper, all right. Same T-shirt and shorts, same ponytail. Sneakers, no socks. He could also see the gray Toyota pickup parked on the grass in the backyard.

"Good girl, Goldie!" Back on his feet, the kidnapper tried to reach for the loose weapon. Sam hooked the crook of Able around the man's ankle and yanked his foot out from under him. Falling on his face this time, the perp bellowed, "You friggin' creep!" While Sam picked up the gun, Goldie placed both front paws on the man's upper back.

Sam shoved the gun in the perp's face. "Where's the boy?"

"Screw you!"

"Have you ever been torn apart by a dog?" asked Sam, holding two fingers in Goldie's line of sight. "One command is all it takes."

The dog obliged with her most ferocious growl. Little did the perp know that golden retrievers are incapable of inflicting that kind of pain, but Goldie proved to be quite an actress. And the dash of Doberman sprinkled a pinch of aggression.

"Okay, okay! He's locked in the bedroom with some toys. He ain't harmed. We didn't do nothin' to him."

"Where's the bedroom?" asked Sam.

"On the other side of the house," the perp said, lifting his head slightly and rubbing the bloody scrapes on his left cheek.

"Hey, Joe," yelled a male voice at the back door. "Where the hell you at?"

"Who's that, and is he armed?" whispered Sam.

"It's my friend Frank, and I don't know whether he has his gun with him. It may be in the car, but I ain't sure. This whole thing was his idea."

"Yeah, sure. Tell him everything's okay."

"Everything's okay, Frank," Joe yelled back. "I'm getting something out of the car."

"Tell him you need some help out here," ordered Sam. "Stay, Goldie. Keep him there."

"Hey, Frank. I could use a little help out here," yelled Joe.

They heard the screen door slam shut and work boots clomping down three wooden stairs. Sam backed up a few feet, concealing himself behind a corner of the bungalow.

Frank was a slouching, skinny guy with a shaved head, receding chin, and weasel blue eyes. "What the hell, man? Wha...wha...what're you doing lying there and where'd that goddamn mutt come from?"

Sam stepped forward and pointed the gun at the skinhead. "Put your hands up."

"Where'd you come from?"

101

"I'm your worst nightmare," said Sam as he frisked Frank for a weapon. He found none and decided from the slurred speech that Frank was zoned out on pot or maybe a stronger drug.

Four unmarked police cars drew up to the curb. Flinging doors open, several officers emerged with Detective Mitch and FBI Agent Manning. They immediately spotted Sam and the kidnappers in the driveway behind the Honda. Frank turned halfway around and tried to run toward the backyard, but all he could manage was a pathetic shuffle. An officer easily caught up and cuffed his wrists behind his back.

Sam ordered Goldie to back off. She obeyed, but looked up at him like "Where's my reward?" Sam didn't happen to have a Milk Bone on him.

Another officer hoisted Joe to his feet and cuffed him. Joe glared at Sam. "Bastard! Look what you did to my face," he whined. The blood had already dried.

"You poor guy," muttered the officer with a suppressed grin. The two officers arrested the men for kidnapping—and more—and read them their rights.

Mitch and Agent Manning entered the house from the back door and found the bookbag stuffed with the money under the kitchen table. But the money wasn't important right now. They began searching the house, which didn't take long; it had only four rooms.

"Hey, Sam?" Mitch called out as he returned to the driveway. "We searched the house. The boy's not here."

"What?" Sam refused to believe it. He hauled himself up the steps after Mitch, who pointed out the door they had opened to the room where Paulie had been held. He saw a twin bed with rumpled sheets shoved up against an open, unscreened window.

"My God, Mitch!" said Sam, his throat nearly closing up. "Paulie's only four, but—"

"Damnit!" said Mitch. "How could we have missed this? Naw, he couldn't have jumped out the window, could he?"

"Yeah, probably," Sam said. "He's quite an athletic little kid, but he might be hurt. It's about a five-foot drop. We'd better start looking outside."

The two police cars carrying the kidnappers had already sped off to the station.

Sam bumbled out the front door, wondering what exactly he should do next. Blame himself, for one thing. *This is all my fault. It's not my case. I should've waited for backup.*

Mitch and Manning had been prowling around the backyard. They reappeared without the child. Joining Sam on the sidewalk, they were about to start searching the neighbors' yards.

Sam suddenly shouted, "Hey! Where's my dog? She's gone!" The three men, in unison, looked to their right. With a shock, they witnessed Goldie galloping down the narrow sidewalk—in pursuit of Paulie. The boy was running his little legs off, crying, "Mommy, Mommy!" Goldie charged just past him and jerked to a stop, effectively blocking the child's path. She lowered herself down, head up, paws forward. Paulie recognized her from their game in the park. He flopped down on the sidewalk, sobbing, and buried his face in her thick fur. She licked his forehead patiently, as if this whole scene was scripted and she was just acting out her part.

Mitch and Manning raced to them. Arriving, Mitch called Douglas and Cynthia Fong, who estimated they would arrive in fifteen minutes. Mitch then called in a report of success to HPD.

Weeping wasn't normally in Sam's repertoire, but as he ski-walked down the block to greet his heroic partner, tears of joy came.

* * * *

Around nine o'clock that night, Sam was sprawled out on his couch watching *NCIS* and devouring slices of leftover pizza, washing them down with Miller Lite. Goldie had inhaled her supper and canine bacon treats and was zonked out on the rug, when the phone rang.

It was Mitch. He and Manning had interrogated the two kidnappers separately. Both were jobless and broke. The house belonged to Frank's aunt and uncle, who were off-island for a three-week vacation. He and Joe had read a newspaper article about Douglas Fong donating two million dollars to his prep school alma mater. They figured he'd be good for the ransom. "Hey, man," Joe had said, "what's two hundred thou to a guy who can give away two mil?" They had planned to let the little boy go, but didn't have a plan for how and where.

"That's great news, Mitch."

But the detective wasn't finished. He chewed Sam out for attempting to rescue Paulie without backup. Sam knew he should let it go. Of course he was wrong. Still, he couldn't resist: "But I did have backup. Goldie saved my *'ōkole* just fine.

§

Episode Eight
A Walk in the Dark

KIANAH NAHOE HEARD FOOTSTEPS FALLING IN BEHIND HER.
Quickening her pace down Pensacola Street, she glanced
over her shoulder for the second time, yet each time she
looked, the footsteps stopped, and no one was there. *Someone's
following me.* She'd felt it twice the previous week—and ignored it.
Tonight, after leaving her office at 8:30, she quickened her stride to
her car in the Young Street lot. Not so easily in heels, even if they
were only mid-high. She'd always considered Honolulu a safe city.
But not tonight. She'd figured stalkers were generally benign—
heard and not seen—that is, until it was time for their mischief.
And that's exactly what she was afraid of. *But who? And why me?*

Kia didn't look the part of a fearful female, nor did she usually feel like one. Her daily wardrobe gave her a professional, no-
nonsense look, today in a gray suit with skirt reaching just above
the knees. She tightened the grip on her briefcase handle as she
passed Auntie Pasto's restaurant. For a split second she thought
of ducking inside and ordering lasagna, anything, just to throw
off whoever it was, but she was dead tired, anxious to get home.
Most of the other businesses along Pensacola had closed for the
night. No surprise there. Luckily, the traffic light turned green. She
crossed the street, continuing to pursue her over-the-shoulder vigi-
lance. Twice she caught a tall figure on the side of Pensacola she'd

just left, moving parallel to her, slipping from the shadowed doorway of the cookie shop to the darkened Korean lunch place. *That proves it. I'm being stalked. When I get home I'll call Sam. He'll know what to do.*

Ironic, isn't it? she thought. Kia had ended their loving marriage under the cruelest of conditions when Sam became unfit to live with. Yet now, even with his disability, she found herself depending on him.

As she reached her Mini Cooper, she assumed the stalker was still tailing her, but she resolved not to turn her head one more time. *Maybe my fear is giving him an ego trip.* She slid into her car, locked the doors, and sped off. In ten minutes she'd reached the safety of her condo and pressed the remote to raise the garage gate. She loved the security of the high-rise on Kanunu Street.

Kia stepped out of the elevator on the third floor and reached in her purse for the apartment keys. No need; the door flew open. Peggy had heard her mother in the hall fumbling for the keys. "Hi, Mom, I already ate, but your supper's in the microwave. Want me to turn it on?"

"Yes, sweetie, I'm starved." Setting her briefcase down in the front hall, Kia managed a quick hug for her child, then flopped into a chair at the kitchen table. "Sorry I'm late, but where's Ms. Dana? I know I left the office a little later than I expected to, but she couldn't stay another half hour 'til I got home?"

"She had some kind of lecture series at nine for the whole week," said Peggy. "I told her you'd be home soon and I'd be okay alone for so little time."

"Peggy, you know I'm not happy about that. I expect Ms. Dana to be more responsible. And you're too young to be left alone, especially at night."

"Mom, that isn't fair. You treat me like a child." Peggy tossed her head. "I'm not too young. I'll be thirteen in September."

Kia, too worn out to argue, couldn't help but notice that her daughter was turning into a younger version of herself: expressive eyes, budding breasts and curving hips, and just old enough to debate with an exasperating sense of logic.

At the microwave Peggy poked in two minutes and waited for the beep. Wearing oven mitts, she carried the casserole to the table, which she'd set for her mother. Her voice softened. "What's wrong, Mom? You look like you've had one long, miserable day."

Kia slid out of her suit jacket and tossed it over an empty chair. "It was a long day," she said, "but that's not what I'm worried about. Remember last week when I said I thought someone was following me after work? It happened again tonight. I'm wondering if I'm being stalked. In fact, I'm pretty sure I am." Kia threw in a few details, but tried not to get overly explicit so she wouldn't frighten Peggy. "I was too far away to see him clearly, except that he was tall and wore dark clothes."

"That *is* creepy, Mom. Shouldn't you be calling the police?"

"And tell them what, dear? I have no proof. They'll think I'm a Nervous Nellie, imagining things." She opened the fridge, pulled out a half-bottle of White Zinfandel, and poured up to the brim of a stemware wine glass.

"Mom, there must be something you can do."

"I suppose I could put your father on the case now that he's a PI. I'll give him a call after I eat. By the way, were there any calls for me today?"

"Not really."

"Not really? What does that mean?" Kia's fork stopped halfway to her mouth.

"Well, our landline phone rang several times this afternoon, but each time I picked it up and said hello, no one answered, although I could hear someone breathing at the other end."

"How many times did this happen?"

"Four, I think. It happened once on my iPhone too."

Under her white blouse, the hairs on the back of Kia's neck tingled. "That's weird," she said. "I've had a few like that in my office over the past few days." She squashed her real feelings. *Where would he have gotten our home phone number? We're not in the phone book. And Peggy's iPhone? This is getting seriously scary. It's like a mounted attack on us.*

* * * *

In a remote neighborhood of Kaimuki, under a misting sky, Sam settled with his latest fare. He frowned. *A real cheapskate, a ten percent tipper.* On the dash, the red open-door icon popped up. He climbed out and re-slammed the rear door the passenger had left ajar.

The digital clock read 9:05 p.m. Sam hadn't been back to this neighborhood in years. There wasn't any need to—there just wasn't anybody left. As he settled back into the driver's seat, an eerie thought tugged at him, causing him to swerve the cab out of the U-turn it had started. Braking mid-road, Goldie cocked her head, which he chose to interpret as an approving look—that whatever he was doing was okay with her. So he swung the wheel true once more, continued on for two blocks, and turned into a cul-de-sac. He parked at the second-last house, across the street from what had once been the Nahoe family dwelling. As he turned off the engine, a smothering feeling of dejection swept over him. The house that stood there now looked neat and well-built, even in the dark under the pale beam of a streetlight.

His forehead began to throb. Was it a sinus headache coming on or the painful memories of the rain-soaked ruins, the charred planks picked clean of anything of value? He and his siblings had been adopted by their kindly grandparents on his mother's side. He'd been only nine years old, reading a comic book in the living room when the fire struck. His ten-year-old brother, Solomon, had been playing with matches in the garage next to a leaking gasoline can—and lost his life. The rest of the family escaped, but his eleven-year-old sister, Eva, got third-degree burns on her face and forearms. The fire demolished everything the family owned. His grandparents never forgave themselves for leaving their young child unsupervised in the garage. A decade later, they died within two years of each other, broken-hearted, in their fifties.

Goldie saw the tears on her master's cheeks and began to whine. Sam leaned over and hugged his best friend and partner.

Then he looked toward the sky and shouted, "Why? Why were they all taken from me?" His excursion through the dreaded past was blessedly interrupted by his phone. He'd recently installed a Bluetooth hands-free setup on the dashboard. The call was from a former customer on Pahoa Avenue needing a ride to a party in Hawai'i Kai.

While conveying the Asian couple to their destination, his phone beckoned once more. His daughter.

"Hi, Daddy, Mom told me to call you."

"Hey, Peggs. How's my sweetheart tonight? Where am I? Passing Koko Head Marina with a fare. Then Goldie and I will head home. Your mother? Put her on. Love ya."

"Hey, Kia. Hold on two minutes, I'm with passengers," said Sam, as he dropped them off and received a sizable tip.

"Hi, I'm back." With engine running, he remained at the curb. "What's up?...A stalker? You actually saw him? By the way, are you sure it's a *he*?...Phone calls too? That's not good. Has anyone new or strange recently come into your life, like trouble with a neighbor in your condo?...How about a disgruntled client? I know that's the reason you became an estates attorney rather than a criminal lawyer. You don't need threats of revenge, especially with Peggy in our lives. Another question: Have you ever felt vulnerable walking to work from the Young Street lot?...No?"

Sam listened. *What to do?* "If it happens again tomorrow, I can start a photo surveillance and maybe identify your stalker. All I'd need from you is a phone call an hour before you leave the office, so I can be in place before he shows up....No, you may not know where I'll be. I can't have you tipping off my presence. Just know I'll be there for you if you need me. Goodnight and hugs and kisses for you both."

In ten minutes, heading west, Sam pulled off Kalaniana'ole Highway and turned up the hill onto Wa'a Street. His first-floor apartment was one of the rare ones in town allowing a big dog—in a single-family home that had been divided into three units. The amiable landlord's only stipulation: "The dog has to be polite." No problem there. Once inside, Sam raided the front hall closet for his camera equipment. The EF-S 18-to-200-millimeter lens threaded neatly into his Eos Rebel T3i camera, setting it to handle telephoto shots. He set the backpack containing the camera equipment and spare memory cards by the front door to take out to the cab in the morning. He hadn't wanted to put additional pressure on Kia, but he'd been wondering for a while now why she had to work so late so often. He guessed, *Must be she has partner ambitions.*

* * * *

On Tuesday evening, Kia's call reached Sam at 7:30, an hour before she planned to leave the office. It was already dark. He knew his ex-wife's route to the car, so he backed the cab into a parking stall on the Diamond Head side of Pensacola. He steadied the long-lens camera on the open window ledge and waited for Kia and her shadow to show.

At 8:43, she crossed over Beretania to the pertinent block of Pensacola, walking toward where Sam had positioned himself. He periodically adjusted the lens so the image included a sharp shot of Kia and the corner where she'd previously crossed. When she had reached a position nearly opposite his cab, a tall figure stepped out of a doorway and fell in behind her, about thirty yards back. Sensing him even at that distance, she whipped around to force a confrontation. At this point she assumed it was a man—in a black hooded sweat jacket. Agile enough to evade her, he ducked behind the wide trunk of a Chinese banyan tree.

Sam zoomed in and began tracking him, but the hood hid most of the man's face. A hawk nose and a quarter of a hairy cheek were all he could capture on camera. When the hooded one passed a lamp-lit trash receptacle, Sam made a mental note of the stalker's height, weight, and build, but there was nothing obvious he could pinpoint about either the stride or carriage.

Kia turned onto Young Street and disappeared from view. Soon afterward, the stalker did the same. Sam quickly packed his gear, piled it in the cab's trunk, and ski-walked to the corner. He saw Kia hurrying along a block away, but there was no sign of the stalker. Sam followed a few steps until she climbed into her Mini and drove off toward home.

* * * *

On Wednesday the unnerving telephone barrage continued at Kia's apartment and office. She left work earlier that night, about seven, when the sun had just set. Sam left his cab and positioned himself around the corner along the hedges on Young, a much more mobile station. With the camera strung around his neck, he used a shorter lens, figuring on the element of surprise, but the target didn't show. On Thursday night, he used the same strategy, At 8:55 he came face-to-face with the hooded one. He snapped the picture all right, but the stalker reacted so fast that the live image had no chance to register in Sam's mind. The stalker spun about and disappeared back down Young, sprinting like an athlete past the Goodwill drop-off.

Sam jerked to a stop under a streetlight, resigned to the reality of his physical limits. But never mind. Checking out the picture on the digital camera's small screen, he assured himself that he had an image to work with—a scruffy face with an unkempt frizzled chin. No one he recognized, but at least a face to show Kia.

* * * *

The next morning, Thursday, Sam used his police alumnus influence and PI credentials at Hawai'ian Telcom to order taps on all of Kia's phones, so that the caller's origin might be traced. Next, he dropped in for a consultation at his ex-wife's office. When he showed her the shot, she just shook her head, her shoulders slumping in defeat.

Sam refused to give up. "Someone you represented maybe? You could have lost the case. Think back," he urged.

Kia straightened up and adjusted the collar of her white blouse as she launched into a more analytical mood. "I haven't lost that many cases, and it's those losses that I remember best. No, I don't think so."

"What about the wins?" Sam pressed. "There's always a

loser in every dispute. Anything there?"

"Nothing off the top of my head. I'd have to go through at least thirteen years of case files."

"Then do it. Look for big money lost or even a jail term involved."

"Okay," she said, relieved to have a concrete assignment. "I'll let you know if I find anything."

"Me too. See ya." He threw her a two-fingered kiss from across the desk and left. She noticed with surprise that he was getting somewhat nimbler, moving just a tad faster.

Sam drove back to the apartment to pick up Goldie and together they conveyed fares across the city of Honolulu for the rest of the day.

* * * *

It wasn't until five in the afternoon on Friday that he got a call from Danny Oshiro. Early that morning Sam had sent him an email with the stalker's picture and asked him to run an ID on it against local motor vehicle licenses. The detective had come up with a facial recognition hit. The man's name was Roger Okamalu, a thirty-five-year-old local. When Danny checked for a criminal record, a lone drunk-and-disorderly charge was all he found.

"Thanks, Danny," said Sam. "Do you have an address for him?"

Sam wrote it down, and stuffed the paper snippet into his sport shirt pocket.

"By the way, Sam, has this stalker broken the law yet?" Danny asked.

"I'd say so. I've got multiple shots on magnetic media cards of him following Kia."

"But that's only circumstantial," reminded Danny.

Sam protested. "Put that together with the phone harassment and what do you have?"

"Still only circumstantial, pal. You said the calls were anonymous. Does Kia have Caller ID?"

"No," Sam replied. "She's been meaning to get it, but no."

"He might have a legitimate reason for contacting your ex-wife. Of course, he should make an appointment to see her in her office."

"Right," said Sam. "Then why did he run from me when I took his close-up picture?"

"He probably doesn't know who you are, and you might have frightened him with the picture-taking."

"Then what are we supposed to do?"

"I know Kia's an attorney. Let her get a restraining order against this man."

"Thanks for your help, Danny. I owe you one."

Sam pushed the disconnect button on the dashboard cell phone and sat back to think. *It's Friday. Five-thirty. Kia can't possibly get a restraining order until next week at the earliest. What can I do in the meantime? Would Roger Okamalu have the balls to stalk her tonight, now that we have a picture of him? Does he have any way of knowing that every phone call he makes to one of Kia's numbers piles up harassment evidence against him?* Sam decided to check out the address Danny had given him, but first he took Goldie to the Itchy Butt for takeout supper to eat in the cab: a *loco moco* and a bowl of chili with rice for himself. He suppressed a spasm of guilt for once again filling his partner up with people food. "An absolute no-no!" the vet had told him. "Too much salt and fat and starch for a dog." Once again Sam resolved to feed her properly next meal.

The Okamalu address was a modest two-story home nestled deep in Palolo Valley, a vast community surrounded by the thickly forested Ko'olau Mountain Range. Making a U-turn, he parked across the street a few houses away, where he could keep an eye on the place. He unhooked the harness and took Goldie for her call-to-nature walk, edging close enough to the house to see a light on in the rear, probably in the kitchen. An older-model Volvo sat, hood facing up, in the steep driveway. Sam smirked. It was simple justice that Goldie deposited her calling card on the tiny front lawn. He refused to feel civic-minded today, even though the law said he should be armed with a baggie and scoop.

Back inside the taxi, he continued his stakeout.

At 6:15 Roger left the house, climbed into the Volvo, and drove out of the valley. At Eleventh Street he entered H-1 West into the usual stop-and-go traffic during the evening rush hour. Sam followed a few cars behind. When the Volvo turned off at the Wilder Avenue exit, Sam suddenly realized that the perp was not headed for Pensacola and Young streets, but just three blocks from Ala Moana Center, near the apartment where Kia and Peggy lived. With Kia still at work, that meant Peggy would be home, possibly alone. *Is my precious Peggs in grave danger? What is this bastard up to?*

The Volvo parked on Kanunu Street in front of a fire hydrant directly across from the high-rise, but kept its engine running. Sam found a space two doors away. *As long as the Volvo engine runs,* Sam reasoned, *the guy has no intention of going inside.* But within minutes an adjacent parking space opened up with a Home Depot delivery truck pulling out. The Volvo re-parked and shut off its engine.

Show time, Sam knew.

Okamalu left the car, crossed the street, and stopped at the intercom beside the condo's front door. Sam and Goldie were only a dozen feet behind when they heard him announce "Delivery, UPS." A long buzz followed with an automated voice reciting "Access Granted."

Sam reached out and grabbed the door before it closed completely, but didn't re-open it all the way until Okamalu stepped into the elevator.

Eyeing the fire door to the left of the lobby, Sam headed straight for it and accessed it using the entrance fob he still carried. Inside, he faced a staircase with a wrought-iron banister. He urged Goldie up the stairs. She charged ahead, having no idea how far to climb, but gleeful and eager to help. Sam grimly placed Cane and Able in his left hand, clutched the banister with his right, and hauled himself up step by step. When he could see that the dog had reached the third-floor landing, he called, "Goldie, stop!" She sat down panting, pink tongue hanging out, waiting for her pal to join her.

Pushing the landing fire door ajar, Sam had a view down the long hall to number 307, Kia's unit. Okamalu stood in front of it, dressed in his black hooded sweat jacket and cargo pants. His hands gripped what looked like a metal box about a foot long. He knocked and waited for a response. Apparently, Peggy did respond, because Sam heard him say, "UPS delivery, got a package for you." A few seconds later he spoke in a stern, gruff voice. "I can't leave it, you gotta sign for it."

Sam swung the fire door away, and he and Goldie rushed to 307, but before they were able to get there, the apartment door had opened, closed, and self-latched again. Sam's heart hammered inside his broad chest. Okamalu was inside, and they weren't.

"Peggy, it's Dad. Let me in!"

Peggy screamed, then uttered a muffled word that sounded like "Daddy."

Sam pounded and Goldie barked. He still had his keys and entrance fob from before the divorce, clipped to the ring on his belt. The split had hit him so hard he just couldn't part with them. He fumbled for the right key, slipped it in the lock, and released the door. He and Goldie lunged inside. Four feet away, Sam's worst nightmare was confirmed. Okamalu held his daughter captive with his arm in a chokehold around her neck. His free hand held a hypodermic syringe to her neck. Sam figured that's what had been in the box. Peggy's normal high color had turned ashen. She stood frozen, in her after-school shorts and T-shirt, yet her eyes were watchful, trusting her father.

"Stay back or I'll use it."

"What's in it?" Sam asked quietly, surprising himself.

Okamalu didn't respond.

Sam held up two fingers to Goldie as he took another step forward and to the left to see better. Goldie circled slowly around to the right, growled, and bared her teeth.

"Stop!" cried Roger. "Don't come any closer, or she gets it. And get that goddamn dog away from me." His head swiveled back and forth between them. Sam could almost read the man's mind, vacillating between using the syringe and giving up the only deterrent he had to stop Sam and the dog.

Another small step. And another. Sam and Goldie approached on either side. Yet another step and they were both within arm's reach. Roger swung the needle away from Peggy's neck and tried to stab Sam, who sidestepped the move and held up one cane as a parrying weapon. Sam clenched his fist twice in plain sight of the dog. Goldie was now close enough. She clamped her teeth around Roger's right ankle. Howling with pain, he released Peggy. She spun about and started kicking his bare shins, her flip-flops not so much hurting as distracting. He waved the needle arm in an arc above his head, but Sam was quicker. Dropping the cane in his right hand, he grabbed Roger by the wrist and wrestled him to gain control of the syringe. Without the syringe threat, the attacker became the victim. No match for Dad, dog, and daughter.

Sam held his arm high, clutching the syringe in his fist. "Okay, Roger, one more move and I'll plunge this thing into your neck."

Roger stopped in his tracks, but Goldie kept her teeth clenched on his ankle until Sam shoved a straight-back chair under his knees, forcing him to sit. Sam gave Goldie the clap-hands-let-go signal, and only then did she release her grip on the raw and bleeding bare ankle.

"Peggy, get me some rope or duct tape, whatever's closest while I call the police." He yanked his smart phone out of his jeans pocket.

Seeing Sam's right hand occupied, Roger leaned forward to make a new move of his own, but Goldie, being a dog with innate initiative, growled again and showed her teeth without being signaled. Roger shrank back into the chair.

Sam speed-dialed Danny. The detective promised to send in the cavalry.

Peggy emerged from the kitchen. "Will these do?" she asked with a nervous giggle. She held up a pair of Sam's old handcuffs that he'd left behind in the apartment.

"You bet, sweetheart," replied the proud father. "How about you call your mother now. Tell her that all of us are safe and unharmed." Sam clamped the manacles behind Roger's back, then stood squarely in front of the perp and demanded, "Why?"

"Why what?" Roger mumbled and turned his face away.

"Look at me, damn it!" Sam flipped the perp's hood off, revealing disheveled hair, then grabbed the prickly chin and yanked his head up. "What's this all about? What have you got against my wife and daughter?"

Roger knew he'd reached the end of the line. "Four years ago last month, Kianah Nahoe stole my father's inheritance from me and gave it to my stepsister, Polani. It belonged to me. I had a right to it. That bitch of a lawyer mixed up what Papa intended and convinced the stupid probate judge to give everything to Polani."

"Just how did she do that?"

"After Papa died, I sued Polani over the will. He had left everything to her. Kianah was her lawyer and twisted all the words around so I didn't get a friggin' thing. Polani wasn't even related to Papa! I'm the son, his blood relation, and I was broke. I had a little daughter, Carlotta. She got real sick and died because I couldn't afford proper medical care. She was only three! I wanted Kianah to know what that felt like." Roger hung his head and started to sob.

* * * *

An hour and a half later, the police had come and gone, taking Roger Okamalu in fresh cuffs with them. Kia burst in. "Is it all over?" she asked, gasping.

"Yes. He's in police custody," Sam replied.

"Thank God!" Kia said. She hugged Peggy—and Sam, too, then bent down to hug Goldie, who gave her a slurpy kiss.

Dropping into an armchair, Kia took a deep breath and told the whole story. "Yesterday, after reviewing my files, I remembered more about the case. Polani was the devoted caregiver to Roger's father for over two years. His father had cancer. During that period, Roger lived by the bottle, an alcoholic, who completely abandoned his own father. Not knowing he even had a granddaughter, the grateful old man clearly wanted Polani to have everything. I don't know why Roger put the blame on me. I do feel sorry for him, though. Losing a child that way, in fact, any way at all, is a tragedy."

It was time for Sam and Goldie to leave, but not before another round of embraces.

"Does this mean you two are gonna get back together?" asked Peggy hopefully.

Sam's stomach muscles froze as he looked to Kia for the answer.

With a sly smile, she said, "The jury's still out."

§

Episode Nine

Peggy and Goldie

P EGGY HAD ATTAINED THE PROMISING AGE OF THIRTEEN ONLY yesterday and had amassed a serious amount of birthday cash from her loving aunties and uncles. Sam offered to take her to a neighborhood branch of the Pacific National Bank in Honolulu to open her first savings account. With Kia already at work, the task naturally fell to Sam this Monday morning. His time was certainly more flexible.

He left Goldie in charge and parked across the street with all four windows down for fresh air. But Sam's razor-sharp mind was taking a momentary holiday. He was so focused on his mission with his daughter that he absent-mindedly released Goldie from her harness.

Peggy pranced along, feeling quite grown-up. Her braids bobbed up and down on her back. She was wearing one of her new birthday outfits: pearl-gray miniskirt, pink shirt, black-and-pink patterned leggings, and sturdy high-top charcoal-gray sneakers with pink laces. At 8:40 Peggy pushed through one of the two glass doors and held it for her dad.

"Thanks, Peggs," he said. But the moment he stepped inside, his body stiffened. Something about the place felt wrong. A deathly silence hovered over the low-ceiling lobby with its recessed lights and tasteful decor. There wasn't a single customer at the four

119

wood-paneled teller stations. Stranger still, there were no tellers at their stations behind the counters.

Sam heard heavy footsteps and slowly turned his head. Two men wearing nylon stocking masks stepped out from behind him. Both were dressed entirely in black. The shorter of the two held a Glock 9mm and wasted no time sticking it into Sam's back. He felt it pressed hard against his white polo shirt. Suddenly, he was shoved forward with such force that he fell on one knee.

"Hey!" he shouted. Still clutching Cane and Able, he dragged himself up to a standing position once more.

The shorter man was built like a hippo, squat, no-necked, and swaggering. He issued drill-sergeant orders to his partner, a towering, beefy islander who hovered close by. "Toma," said the hippo, "take his cell, and the kid's too, if she has one. I'm locking this troublemaker up with the others. We'll take the kid hostage."

"Aw, Boss," Toma muttered. "That's crazy."

Boss ignored his accomplice. He did not take well to being challenged.

Sam didn't give a damn whether there was a gun in his back or not. "No!" he bellowed. "You're not taking my little girl. Take me instead. I can't give you any trouble. You can see I'm crippled. Don't hurt her. She's only thirteen, for God's sake." He half-turned and whipped Cane upward to swat Toma in the head. But Toma grabbed it from him and returned the favor by striking it against the side of Sam's skull, sending a lightning bolt of pain through Sam's head. Toma tossed the cane far out of reach.

Boss shoved Sam forward, stumbling and dizzy, toward the far side of the lobby, to a door marked Manager. The key was in the lock. Boss opened the door and pushed his victim inside. Sam's bass voice thundered: "You do one thing to harm my little girl, and I swear you're a dead man." The second half of his threat was muffled by the door slamming shut on his words. He heard the key turn in the lock.

Sam fell to the floor, still grasping his one cane, his long legs splaying out like a spider's. The left side of his head ached, not so much from the blow, but from knowing he was totally helpless. *A lotta good my PI license is doing me now. I can't even protect my own child.* He hated that he was getting a paunch, softening up from a lack of exercise. With high hopes, he had haunted a fitness center for six months, working out on a stationary bike and treadmill, but his back ached even more after each session. The simple act of walking more than a hundred yards, even though he could move more quickly than two years ago, caused too much pain. *And now, how the devil am I going to get out of this small, windowless office?*

Sprawled on the floor, he saw that he was trapped with four other victims, all wearing name tags: three females—tellers, he assumed—and a young Asian man in a light-blue shirt and tie, with a nametag reading "Alan Yoshita, Manager." Alan sat at his desk. and two of the tellers, although tense with fright, sat in the chairs across from him, as if they were all conducting a financial transaction on an ordinary day. The third teller, a fresh-faced new-hire in a pants suit and suede boots, crouched on the floor against the left wall, legs drawn up to her chest, arms hugging her knees.

The manager rose up from his swivel chair. Rounding his desk, he bent over to help Sam to a sitting position.

After introducing himself, Sam asked, "What happened?"

"We all arrived about the same time, a little before eight," Alan said. "A half-hour later, the two men appeared out of nowhere. The short one forced the tellers at gunpoint to hand over all the cash in the drawers. I would guess they got about fifteen thousand. Maybe less. The tall guy stuffed the money in a gym bag. I tried to hightail it into my office to call the police, but didn't get a chance."

"Did they make you hand over your wallets and cell phones?" Sam asked.

"Not our wallets. Maybe they figured they'd get more money out of the bank drawers. They did take our cells. The big guy threw them into the bag with the money."

"Mine too," Sam said.

Ashen-faced, Alan defended himself. "The short one's a real

bully. He followed me to the office and held his gun on me, forcing me to hand over the key. Then the robber cut the wire to the landline on my desk."

"That's bad," Sam said.

Out in the lobby, Peggy had witnessed her father manhandled and locked away. Her sturdy body trembled with fear. The gun threatening Sam had kept her submissive, but when she saw Boss tuck the weapon into his pants belt, she started screaming. He tried to grab her by one arm, but she kicked hard at his shins.

Boss yelled, "Toma, gimmee the money and hang onto this rotten brat. I'm going out to start the truck."

Toma tried again. "Aw, Boss, what the hell do we need her for? She's just a little kid. We got the money. Let's just get outta here."

"I told you she's gonna be our hostage, you idiot. If the police chase us they won't shoot if we've got the girl." He grabbed the gym bag and bulled out the door ahead of Toma and Peggy.

Outside the bank, they moved toward a maroon sparkling-new pickup. It was intentionally parked with the bed gate dropped, so that it cast the rear license plate in a dark shadow. Toma's sweaty left hand held Peggy's arm above the elbow—rather half-heartedly, she noticed. She lowered her head, opened her mouth wide, and chomped down on the fleshy part of his hand. He yelped and yanked it away. Placing one arm under her knees, he hefted her off her feet, carried her the few steps to the truck, and set her down. She screamed, but no pedestrians appeared to be in sight. With both feet free, she kicked hard, but couldn't reach his shins. He was huge and too strong. He swung open the door behind the driver's side and lowered her onto the floor. Slamming the door shut, he lumbered around the truck and climbed into the front passenger seat. Boss started the engine.

Lying on the carpeted floor, Peggy yearned to just let go and sob with frustration. But with the grit inherited from both her parents, she held her emotions in check and began to calculate. To her surprise, she had been left unrestrained. She climbed up onto the soft seat, which smelled of fresh new leather, and let her brain shift into overdrive. Toma—she'd listened carefully and remembered his name—had not hurt her. He had actually set her down quite gently. She couldn't decide: should she buckle herself in or not? If she didn't, maybe she could escape. She reached for the door handle, but heard a loud click. The handle wouldn't budge. Boss must have read her thoughts and locked her in.

She thought again how odd it was that there were no pedestrians on the sidewalk. Still, her kicking and screaming had not gone entirely unnoticed. Goldie had seen her beloved Peggy in trouble. Sam's cab was parked at the curb several cars behind the truck. Happily free of her harness, the retriever squeezed her sixty-five-pound body through the driver's-door open window and hit the street galloping. A car behind her screeched to a stop.

"Dumb dog!" the driver yelled.

Goldie had heard the pickup engine start and reached the truck bed just as it began to crawl through congested traffic. The powerful dog's chase momentum, along with her leaping ability, was enough to lift her onto the dropped gate and into the truck bed. Landing on all fours, she slid backward with the truck's forward motion until her clawing, slipping hind legs hung precariously over the gate's edge. Luckily, the pickup slowed, then turned right at the first corner, helping Goldie roll deeper and safer toward the cab. The din of morning rush-hour traffic, and the clattering construction of new luxury high-rises, covered any noise the bank robbers might have heard from the rear. A light rain began to fall. Goldie found shelter under a crumpled blue tarp in the truck bed.

* * * *

Vicky Mateo's dental appointment that morning involved a root canal, so she was a half-hour late to her teller's window at Pacific National Bank. She'd had the manager's permission to be late—that wasn't the problem. She entered an eerily quiet, deserted lobby during regular banking hours with immediate suspicion. Where was everyone? At her station, she opened the cash drawer. It was empty. Chicken-skin covered her bare arms. She automatically reached under the counter and set off the silent alarm, alerting both HPD and the FBI. Then Vicky got bolder and began to explore the empty lobby. She heard muffled noises, crying and shouting, coming from the manager's office.

"Who's in there?" she called.

A jumble of voices yelled back. The deadbolt key was still in the lock. Vicky unlocked the steel door and swung it wide. The three tellers emerged first, showering their coworker with thanks and hugs. Alan kindly helped Sam to his feet. Sam hobbled out on one cane, and gratefully found the other one on the floor against a wall. Just then, two police cars pulled up, and four officers rushed toward the front door.

* * * *

Peggy heard sirens off in the distance. Holding her breath, she silently prayed the police were coming to rescue her. But the sounds grew fainter and fainter. *Maybe they'll rescue Daddy first and then they'll come for me,* she thought. But her hopes soon deflated. Tears welled up under her thick lashes. *Where are these horrible people taking me? How can Daddy find me?*

The truck accelerated as it entered the freeway west. Peggy blinked hard and brushed the tears away. It was time to start thinking. They were driving farther and faster away from town. She wished she'd worn the Timex that Grandma had given her for her birthday. Peggy had thanked her warmly, but didn't admit the truth: that she and her friends never wore watches; they checked the time on their iPhones. The guy called Toma had grabbed her pastel-flowered purse and filched her new iPhone. Kia had been annoyed that Sam was spoiling their daughter with such a lavish birthday gift.

The rain beat down harder now, slapping against the windows. They drove through a farming area with few houses and, off in the distance, herds of cows grazing. Dairy farm country, Peggy guessed. The Wai'anae Mountain Range loomed in the background, shrouded in thick mist. Turning onto a narrow dirt road, the pickup slowed as it passed a ramshackle bungalow, and stopped in front of a huge, weathered gray barn.

Toma climbed out, opened the padlock with a key, and pulled back the wide barn door, which squeaked in protest. Boss maneuvered a three-point turn and backed the truck inside the cavernous space. Toma pulled the barn door shut behind him, and flicked on the light, a bare bulb hanging by a wire from a rafter. Returning to the truck, he swung the back door open. "Time to get out, little girl," he said. He'd planned to lift her off the seat himself, but having carried her once, thought better of it. *That one's strong, prob'ly five feet tall, maybe a hundred pounds.*

Peggy didn't move. She was trying to figure out where she'd be better off. It was stuffy inside the truck. What if they locked her in it? Maybe she'd suffocate. But she wasn't given a choice. Toma nudged her off the seat and let her slide down to the floor on her own.

The moment Peggy landed upright, all four of her limbs started bombarding Toma. Her sneakers' heels pelted his shins. He jumped back, out of her reach. She tripped mid-kick and fell on the straw-covered dirt floor.

The two men had removed their stocking masks. Peggy cocked her head to study them. The bearish, blustery guy, Toma, had a benign round face, matted black hair, and slightly floppy ears with big lobes. Boss, along with his hippo-like girth, had squinting eyes and a fleshy chin. His buzz cut was so short that she could see his pink scalp. *Military?* she wondered.

Toma was the first to speak. "Hey, Boss. What the hell we gonna do wi' this kid? Takin' her was a big mistake. Now she's seen our faces and knows where we hang out, yah?"

"I don't know yet," snapped Boss. "Tie 'er up or something while I think things out."

Toma scowled. "Forget it," he muttered.

"Hey, you guys," Peggy called from her sprawled-out position on the floor. "I can hear you talking about me. I'm only thirteen. How about I just walk away from here with a very, very poor memory? Honest! I could easily forget I ever saw you or this place.

I'm real good at forgetting. I forget my homework assignments a lot. I can get far away from here in a big hurry."

"Shuddup, brat," yelled Boss. Then noticing the contents of one of the nearby stalls, he said, "Hey, Toma, how 'bout the dog cage in the stall over there?"

"Aw, Boss, give it up," said Toma, his voice wavering. "She's not going no place. Why don't we just head up to your house to get somethin' t' eat?"

"Yeah, sure, but we can't just leave the brat running around loose like this." Infuriated by Toma's defiance, Boss resorted to the only move left to him. He pulled out the Glock from his pants belt and waved it in her direction. "Get over there," he said, pointing with his free hand toward the cage.

Peggy walked slowly, dragging her feet, but knowing better than to argue with a gun. She knelt down, ducked her head, and crawled inside. Boss flipped the hasp over the U-bolt, and stuck a bolt through to keep it locked in place.

As her captor walked away, she yelled after him. "Hey, you can't leave me in this thing like some zoo animal. Besides, it's child abuse. My mom's a lawyer, and she'll get after you for this. You'll be sorry."

"Who sez? Yell all you want. Ain't nobody gonna hear you." Boss disappeared out of the barn, slammed the door behind him, and jogged to catch up with Toma.

Peggy felt anger swell inside her as she plopped down cross-legged on the bed of hay, which she found softer than the coarse straw on the barn floor, and surveyed her surroundings. She saw a line of empty stalls—for cows, most likely. The air smelled of stale manure. The rectangular steel cage was actually higher than her head when she was sitting—*made for a Great Dane or some other enormous dog,* she thought. She tried to bend one section. Although she could fit three fingers through the heavy-duty wire mesh, her whole hand could not. Shaking the cage proved unproductive. She could see the bolt, but there was no way she could reach it. *There's room to lie down,* she thought, *but, yuck, I wouldn't want to.* She

126

anchored her back against one side wall and pushed against the opposite wall with her sneakers. Stretching out her legs with all her might slightly bowed the cage, but only momentarily. The mesh was too strong. Frustration and helplessness displaced anger. She felt more afraid and more alone than ever before in her whole life.

But Peggy wasn't alone. The blue tarp in the truck bed began to stir. Goldie had heard all the earlier commotion. Cowering, she stayed hidden, frightened by the men's arguing and Boss's threats. Her dear Peggy's screaming and trying to fight back scared her even more. But now Peggy's protests were too much to bear. Goldie poked her head out and padded to the edge of the truck bed. The pickup's gate was still flat open. She leapt to the straw-covered floor, trotted excitedly toward the cage, and bumped it, causing it to rock slightly off its base.

"Goldie!" In total disbelief, Peggy laughed in spite of herself. "I can't believe it!" As the dog vigorously wagged her tail and licked Peggy's fingers through the mesh, Peggy had an idea. If it was possible for Goldie to rock the cage even slightly off its base, maybe the two of them could rock it back and forth until the cage flopped over. *Maybe if we do it enough, the bolt will fall out. Maybe.* Peggy stretched out both arms, clutched the wire mesh on both her right and left, and started a rocking motion. The cage bottom lifted slightly on both sides, but rocking the heavy cage was hard work. She soon had to stop to rest. All the while she coaxed the golden to join her. "Come on, girl, help me!"

Smart as the dog was, she didn't understand what Peggy wanted from her. Besides, she'd found a toy: a large, dried-out cow pie.

Ewwww. Yuck. Peggy made a face. But this was no time to get distracted. Her lips pressed together with determination—like her keen focus when she was about to kick a goal for her middle-school soccer team. She began to think. Of course—the trick Sam had taught the dog to stop a fleeing crook, opening and closing his left fist in the air. Goldie would pursue and take the crook down by ramming into the back of the knees. In fact, Peggy herself had used it to stop Carly Adams in front of the elevator at Ward.

Fearful that her captors would soon return, Peggy began to rock again—until she got the cage flopping off its base. She yelled to Goldie. "Come!" while opening and closing her left fist. Goldie raised her head, forgot the cow pie, and sprang up. She charged the cage, this time hitting the upper edge with her muscled body. The coincidence of forces was perfect. The cage flopped over on its side. "Good girl, Goldie. You did it. Such a good, good girl."

Peggy's exaggerated praise convinced Goldie that she should repeat what she had done. But now that the cage was already on its side, what was the point? Frantic and discouraged, Peggy failed to notice that the bolt had already worked its way loose and fallen off. She gave up. But Goldie did not. She charged the cage once more and the hasp flipped away, causing the door to swing open.

Peggy crawled out and stood up. She and Goldie started for the barn door to make their escape when they heard footsteps approaching. Peggy spun around for something she could use as a weapon. A rusty pitchfork hung on the wall. She grabbed it and waited.

Toma stepped inside. Peggy was standing behind the open door. With all her strength, she swung the pitchfork in a downward arc and plunged one of the tines through his right calf, piercing his pants leg.

"Yeow!" he roared. Reeling from shock and pain, he tried to grab the pitchfork handle, but stumbled and fell backward onto the floor with a great thud. She saw a paper plate fly out of his other hand and land halfway across the room. A *manapua* rolled off it—a steamed bun filled with sweet *char siu* pork. Toma had brought it from the house for her. Prostrate in agony, he had no idea there was a dog in a far corner, wolfing it down.

"Yo, Toma," called Boss from the driveway. "What the hell are ya doin' in there?"

Peggy was caught between the prone Toma and the threat outside. A pointed gun appeared first as the door creaked open and Boss entered the barn. She wanted to run and took the first two steps toward the row of stalls, but she didn't get far.

"Stop, brat, or I'll shoot."

Quivering, Peggy half-turned to face him. "I'm not going back in that cage, Mr. Boss." Her peripheral vision caught Goldie in the corner, moving silently in the shadows, but managing to stay unseen.

Toma shouted, his squawking voice breaking up in pain. "Hey, Boss! Quick! Get this damn thing outta my leg."

Boss whipped around, still clutching his weapon, and found his partner lying in the straw. He grabbed the pitchfork with his free hand and wiggled it back and forth.

Toma roared, "Yeow! Pull it straight out, fer chrissake, don't rip me!"

With Boss standing over Toma, Peggy signaled Goldie with her left fist one more time. Boss had not yet stuck the gun in his belt. Goldie charged forward and hit him squarely behind the knees, collapsing him over the top of his wounded accomplice.

The gun slid across the floor. Peggy took off after it. Boss rolled off Toma and tried to get to his feet to give chase. But Goldie was on a roll herself. She'd received no signal to stop. She clamped her jaws around Boss's left ankle. He collapsed on his stomach again. Her grip wouldn't allow him to turn face-up.

Peggy bolted forward and quickly picked up the weapon. Trembling, she turned around and pointed it at the two of them. "Mr. Boss, if you think I don't know how to use this, think again. See that Dr. Pepper over there?" She nodded toward a half-crushed can sitting on a wood shelf a few feet away. She pulled the trigger once. The can flew up and landed on the floor.

"Jeezuz," he muttered.

Pointing the weapon at them once more, Peggy appeared outwardly composed, suppressing the cold knot of terror she felt inside. "My dad was a policeman and now he's a private investigator. Empty your pockets and throw everything out in front here." She slapped her leg with her free left hand. Goldie perceived it as a clap, the signal to release Boss's ankle.

Boss hauled himself up to a sitting position, still sore from Goldie's jaws, and tossed out a cell phone, two rings full of keys, a wallet, some coins, and a pocket knife. "That's it," he said.

"You sure?"

"Yah."

"Mr. Boss, now empty Toma's pockets, and add his stuff to the pile," said Peggy. "Maybe you can roll up his pants leg and do something about the wound."

"You sure give a helluva lot of orders for a kid." He pushed Toma's pants leg up to expose the lacerated calf. It was slimy and bleeding, with flecks of rust along the torn flesh. "Hell with that," Boss grumbled. Instead, he fished through his partner's pockets. The pile grew—a second phone, a wallet, a key ring, and a rabbit's foot.

A glittering flash of red caught Peggy's eye. She did a double-take. "My iPhone! Toma, what were you doing with it in your pocket? I thought you put it in the bag with the money."

The massive guy looked peculiarly at odds squirming on the floor.

Peggy felt a spasm of pity. "Sorry I had to do that to you, Toma. But I'm asking you, what were you doing with my phone?"

With a look of hopelessness on his puffy, unshaven face, Toma said, "I was gonna give it to my little girl. I can't afford one. I got laid off."

Peggy understood. *He needed money. So that's why he agreed to go along with the robbery.* But that wasn't her problem. Getting rescued was. She leaned down and scooped the phone up, well aware that her dad no longer had his. She punched in her phone contacts and her mother's cell.

"Mommy!"

"Darling! Are you all right? Where are you?" Kia's voice choked with tears as she kept talking. "Daddy's okay. I'm here with him at the station—with the police and FBI. We're both frantic. I love you, and I'm putting Daddy on."

"Daddy? I'm okay....Really, I'm fine. So is Goldie. She's

here with me....She must've jumped out of the taxi window and into the truck. She's been amazing. Yeah, I'm holding a gun on your two bank robbers. It's Mr. Boss's gun. Daddy, come get us! We want to go home!...Where am I? I don't know. We took the freeway west into farm country. I saw cows grazing. We're in some kind of abandoned dairy barn....Yes, my phone is fully charged. You taught me to always make sure....You did what?"

Sam told her that he had installed the GPS app into her iPhone when he bought it. As he spoke, the police were beginning to track her location.

Leaning against a truck fender to steady her nerve-wracked emotions, Peggy pointed the gun at the men on the floor in front of her.

Boss's hardened look grew slack. It dawned on him how stupid they'd been to leave the truck gate down. *So that's how that miserable cur got on. And it's her dog?*

* * * *

Sam knew it would take at least forty minutes to reach Peggy from HPD headquarters. But he was also with Pop Lione from Robbery. Pop immediately contacted the HPD Kapolei Station on west Oʻahu, less than ten minutes away from her GPS location.

* * * *

Peggy heard the police sirens. Boss had made only one aggressive move, and Goldie had put an end to it with a growl, ear-splitting barking, and feinting a charge at him. Peggy edged around her prisoners and swung the barn door back as three police cruisers entered the dirt road and screeched to a halt in front of the barn. The assault team quickly took charge. With breathless relief, Peggy surrendered Boss's weapon.

One officer cuffed Boss behind his back and read him his Miranda rights. The other officers looked at each other, virtually scratching their heads at this uncommon scene. A young girl—with a golden retriever leaning protectively against her leg—was holding two bank robbers at bay, one with an ugly wound and a rusty pitchfork lying next to him.

But Peggy's conscience wouldn't leave her alone. "Officers," she said, pointing to Toma, "this man is hurt. Could you please call an ambulance for him?"

"On it!" said the closest officer. He knelt down beside Toma, first Mirandizing him, then cuffing him—behind his back wasn't necessary; Toma appeared about to pass out.

While waiting for the ambulance, two officers fixed their attention on the brand-new, flashy pickup. They called in the plates. The truck had been stolen about 4 a.m. that very day from a driveway in Waimanalo, a town on O'ahu's windward side, and reported to HPD by CrimeStoppers. Grand theft auto would be added to the charges of armed bank robbery, hostage-taking, and kidnapping a minor.

Peggy stood just outside the barn door, scanning the long muddy road to the highway. The rain had stopped. A huge smile lit up her face when she saw Sam's Checker Cab approach and brake to a stop. Sam barely had time to hoist himself out when Peggy leaped into his arms. Both father and daughter sobbed with relief as they clung to each other in a tight embrace. For several minutes Peggy couldn't let go of her dad or stop crying. It felt so good to be safe again. And then Kia appeared from the passenger side of the cab and joined the hugging twosome.

The ambulance arrived shortly, and the EMTs strapped the handcuffed Toma to a gurney. As the two felons were about to be taken away, Peggy said, "Daddy, wait. I need to talk to Toma. It's important."

Sam frowned. "Only with me here."

Peggy looked down at the helpless man. "Mr. Toma, you didn't act much like a bank robber. Of course, I don't really know what bank robbers act like. Anyway, how come you were so gentle with me? And you brought me lunch! You sure surprised me."

Woozy Toma whispered, "My little girl's about your age and she's just dying to have a cell phone."

Moments later, just before Sam, Kia, Peggy, and Goldie climbed into the taxi, Peggy grasped her father's hand and squeezed it. "Daddy, when we open my savings account, can we go to a different bank?"

"It wasn't the bank's fault, sweetheart," he said. "But yeah, of course, anything you want."

§

Episode Ten
Second-Story *Moke*

DENSE CLOUDS HID MORE THAN THE FULL MOON HOVERing over Auntie Wila's house. They also hid an intruder lurking among her lush bougainvillea bushes. It was a *moke*—pidgin for a local guy whose idea of fun is to smash someone's kisser.

Auntie Wila Lopeki often struggled with insomnia. But not tonight. At a touch past midnight, she slept under an umbrella of fatigue in her second-floor bedroom. Zonked was more like it. Her nephew, Sam Nahoe, had picked her up after breakfast yesterday for a family picnic at Kaka'ako Waterfront Park and didn't bring her home until bedtime. Oh, she enjoyed being with the younger folks. In fact, it tickled Auntie to note how the divorced couple still found excuses to spend time together.

But for Wila, just turned eight-three, today was long, too long. A wise old bird, she knew she'd done it to herself. Feeling sprightly, she had borrowed Peggy's bicycle for a spin along the park's oceanside promenade—then discovered she was fifty years too late to retrieve her bike-riding skills. Wila was skinny, but strong, with a shriveled face and sharp chin. Recently retired, she'd held a job usually meant for a much younger person. But as a carrier for the *Honolulu Star-Advertiser*, she'd handled the job remarkably well, delivering papers to residents in a city high-rise, starting at 3 a.m. seven days a week.

Auntie didn't hear her bougainvillea trellis complain under the weight of a climbing intruder. The aluminum trellis, leaning against the side of the house, provided a perfect invitation to a skilled climber. Auntie didn't even wake up when the half-open bedroom window slid farther and farther up its tracks to accommodate the intruder's bulk.

This *moke* deftly climbed in, despite his 230 pounds of nasty bulk. This particular low-life had nothing personal against Auntie Wila—only that her modest home looked easy to burgle. At least easier than the more lavish houses he had cased from the street with their security-company stickers on the doors.

The second-story *moke* waited a few moments for his eyes to acclimate to the inside darkness, then strode across the carpeted floor to the mirrored dresser. The shallow top drawers were always the most likely to contain pricey goodies. Silently pulling open the two felt-lined drawers, he flashed a thin Maglite beam over the costume-quality pins, earrings, and necklaces. With a practiced eye, he selected the only piece worth fencing and slipped it into one of his cargo pants pockets. He knew exactly what he wanted, and even that piece was a compromise. He laid the Maglite on the dresser top and slid the two drawers back in place—only the second one required a *skosh* more beef to secure it shut. The slam didn't sound nearly as loud as he perceived it. He turned toward the sleeping figure.

Auntie Wila groaned, mumbled a few unintelligible syllables, and rolled onto her opposite hip. As she flipped over, she threw off the bedcovers, revealing a bony form inside her nightie. The gentle breeze from the open window proved caressing and comfortable, so she slept on undisturbed.

The *moke* waited for the quiet to resume and then returned to the business at hand: the nine deep drawers in the dresser. He rummaged through each one with his bare hands, poking through the petite-sized shorts, tops, jeans, and undies. In the central bottom drawer, he found what he was looking for: a white leather jewelry box with a gold-colored clasp. Pressing the clasp until it noiselessly sprang open, he lifted the hinged top and discovered two tiers of elegant pieces arranged on purple velvet. The mother lode. A finely etched whalebone scrimshaw brooch, a black pearl pendant, and three jeweled rings: an opal surrounded by sapphires; a jade stone set in gold, and a one-karat engagement diamond.

In his excitement, the thief elbowed the Maglite off the dresser top. It thudded to the floor. He cringed and quickly turned to face the bed once more. The small figure lying there didn't seem to be moving at all. In fact, he thought he'd detected a string of snores. He turned back to the dresser, scooped up the entire contents of the case in his large, sausage-like fingers, and shoved the lot into one of his deep pockets. The thief was so exhilarated with his booty that he failed to hear quiet movement in the other part of the room. He tucked the empty jewelry box back into the bottom drawer. Sliding the drawer shut, he stood up and glanced in the mirror. The bed was now empty. Before he had a chance to survey the room, he felt something hard stuck in the middle of his back.

"Reach for the sky!" said a crackling alto voice. "Put your hands in the air. No, don' turn 'round. I got you covered up, yah."

The *moke* looked back into the triple dresser mirror, especially the right-hand section, and discovered a person no more than four-foot-six pressing a rolled-up magazine against his back, trying her damnedest to make him believe she had a gun.

In the darkness of her bedroom, Wila glared up at the thug with a ferocious frown, hoping to scare him away.

The thief then realized the gutsy broad hadn't really thought out this whole confrontation thing. The crack of a vicious smile grew on his lips. In one swift motion, he pivoted to his left and caught the barefoot old lady in the solar plexus with his balled-up fist. Wila's eyes widened and her gaunt cheeks filled with air as he buried his right hand into the braided network of nerves behind her stomach. All eighty-five pounds of Auntie Wila lifted off the floor and flew against the closet door with a bang, slumping to the floor in a posed-like, sitting position. Auntie's eyes slammed shut, and her chin jerked down to her chest, while the old widow's mouth hung slack as a Hawai'ian guitar string.

The *moke* gave her the once-over and discovered a gold wedding band on her left hand. He struggled with the ring until he found a way to wrench it from her scrawny fourth finger. She exhibited no pain and made no noise, so he leaned closer, listened for her breathing, and satisfied himself that she was still alive. Then, back at the dresser, he removed a pair of Auntie's laundered cotton panties and wiped down most of the dark-wood dresser top. Before hurrying to the open window, he scanned the room one last time, then wiggled through the window, wiping the sill from the outside. He tossed the panties inside onto the floor and climbed down the trellis, wedging his sneakers between the bougainvillea vines, and fled into the blackness of night.

* * * *

Sam was almost as fatigued as Auntie Wila from a whole day at the beach park, so in his depth of sleep he could easily ignore his landline phone ringing off the hook. That is, until a sloppy, dribbling tongue sloshed across his cheek and Goldie's malodorous breath assaulted his nose. He awoke with a start and pushed his furry pal's nose out of the way to reach the irritating phone.

"Hello," he grumbled. His eyes strayed to the luminous clock. *Damned robo-Mainlanders calling at all hours.* "Hello, who is this? It's 3:30 in the morning here," he carped when he heard nothing at the other end of the line. Then, listening more intently, he thought he heard a trembling, weak voice say, "Auntie Wila."

"Auntie Wila?" he repeated. "I can hardly hear you. What's wrong?...You've been robbed and beaten? How bad? Do you need an ambulance? No? Are you sure, Auntie?...Put some ice on where it hurts. Have you called the police yet?...Why not?...Okay, we'll be there in a little bit."

Sam hung up the phone and began dressing. As he brought one leg up and twisted his hip forward to pull on a sock, he felt a stinging pain run through his back and torso. He twisted back and forth, moaning with pain. Goldie brought her forelegs up onto the

137

bed in sympathy. Within minutes, the pain eased and Sam finished dressing. He grabbed Cane and Able, and he and Goldie were out the door and on their way to Auntie Wila's place.

* * * *

At 4 a.m. Sam drove into the parking lot at Don Quijote, a huge 24/7 market on Kaheka Street, and slid the taxi into a fifteen-minute space. *Just enough time to pick up a bag of dog food,* he thought. *Auntie Wila can wait that long, but Goldie needs her breakfast.* He ruffled the fur behind her ears.

In his hurry, ski-walking faster than he should have, he accidentally bumped into a stocky woman leaving the store. The bump was enough to dislodge her cloth grocery bag. Fortunately, it dropped straight to the ground without its contents tumbling out. Sam fetched it for her using a neat trick he'd perfected: scooping up the bag's handles in the crook end of Able.

"Sorry, ma'am!"

"Just watch where you're going next time!"

"Yes, ma'am," he replied.

"Mom!" a reproachful voice said. "It's not his fault. The man's disabled. And it's dark out."

The woman harrumphed. "Well, he still should be more careful."

"Oh Mom," returned an embarrassed girl, probably in her mid-teens.

Sam gave the daughter a second look. *Good Lord!* His heart skipped a beat. The girl looked so much like his dead sister, Eva.

Mother and daughter continued to the parking lot. Other nighttime shoppers churned around him, but Sam stood fixed in his tracks. His memory was playing dirty tricks on him again. Eva's burns healed quickly enough over the year after the fire, but not so the scars, which left permanent pale red marks on her cheek and left forearm. With no money to pay for cosmetic surgery, Eva endured her lot quietly, bravely, but three years after the fire she succumbed to pneumonia, caused by an undetected, weakened immune system.

138

With great effort, Sam suppressed the terrible memories. Goldie needed breakfast. Auntie Wila needed him.

* * * *

A half-hour later Sam pulled into Auntie's driveway and crunched to a stop on the gravel surface. He walked across the front lawn, up onto the lanai, and inside through the unlocked door. As he burst into the parlor, Auntie was sitting in her recliner, surprisingly dressed up in a ruffled green muʻumuʻu with yellow and white plumerias. She had a cold pack pressed to her ribs and a bag of frozen peas perched atop her scalp, where it had slammed into the closet door.

Goldie trotted across the floor and circled twice before settling down quietly next to her. Wila buried her hand in the golden's fur, and the two were as one.

Before Sam had a chance to ask, Auntie Wila spilled out all the frightening details of her wee-hour's encounter.

"It'll take a lot mo' den dat to put dis ol' broad outta commish," she said.

"But are you okay, Auntie? That's the most important thing."

"Dat big *moke* took da breath clean outta me, yah. Punched me bad right here." She rubbed her solar plexus with gnarled fingers. "Gotta knot back here too." She bent her head, chin to chest.

He leaned over and saw an inch-long gash of dried blood on her pink scalp between the thinning strands of salt-and-pepper hair. "It's more than a bump, Auntie. You may need stitches. Let me take you to the ER now or Urgent Care tomorrow morning, the one right here in Kalihi."

"No, Sam, you no takin' me anywhere. You clean it fo' me. You good at dat."

Sam knew he'd lost that round. He decided to clean up her wound himself. But first, he whipped out his iPhone. "How about I take a picture of the cut on your scalp? It's proof of what a scumbag the thief was."

"Okay, Sam, honey, I don' mind my head gettin' famous."

Bending her head once more, he tapped his camera function and tapped three times. Goldie took this occasion to remind them how important she was. She reared up on her hind legs, pushed her nose close to Wila, and licked one shriveled cheek.

"Sam, honey, do my ribs too. Dey sure am sore." She lifted her muʻumuʻu up to 'her ribs, where an ugly purple bruise had already formed.

Sam snapped another photo. "Thanks, Auntie, you're being very helpful even if you won't go to a doctor." He gently washed the bloody cut on her scalp, dried it carefully, and covered it with a small antibiotic bandage. Goldie supplied her own brand of first aid with sloppy kisses to the old lady's heavily veined hand as she allowed Sam to minister to her.

"I'm gonna call the police now, Auntie."

She scowled and drew her tiny body erect. "No you don'! *You* I can trust to find my stuff, Sam. But da cops ask too many questions, push lotsa paper, an' do nuthin' no good. I don' want dem poking round my place."

Seating himself in a straight-backed chair next to the recliner, he said, "I know you're all shook up, Auntie, and I would be too, but I gotta know. What did the *moke* take? Anything of value?"

"All my rings, engagement diamond too, and my pearl pendant, and my greaʼ-greaʼ-grandma's scrimshaw brooch. If my *tutu* knew, she roll in 'er grave."

Sam half-reared up out of his chair. "The one with the beautifully carved sailing ship? That's an antique, worth even more than your diamond. And sentimental too. What did this guy look like, Auntie?"

"Like all *moke*, beeeg an' mean wi' lotta black hair in pony tail." Her short arms were stretched as high and wide as they could reach.

"Any tattoos? Scars?"

"No see—too dark."

"I'm going up to your room and have a look around. You

140

stay here." With Cane and Able clutched in his left palm, Sam relied on his right hand and the banister to navigate up the flight to the second floor. Ever-curious and protective, Goldie followed him a few safe feet behind. Inside Wila's compact bedroom, he discovered a smear of blood on the closet door where she'd hit her head. Using his iPhone, he snapped another picture—more evidence. Scanning the rest of the room, he smiled when he saw that Auntie Wila had already made her bed and folded her nightie precisely next to the pillow. He even noted the dust line on the dark-wood dresser top where Auntie had supposedly swiped across it in a hurry.

Nothing else seemed out of place. Then Sam noticed a patch of white cloth lying on the floor next to the window at the same moment Goldie saw it. She trotted to the window and sniffed the cloth a few times before picking it up in her teeth and bringing it to him. The patch of white cloth turned out to be a pair of Wila's panties, soiled with dust—not from being worn. *A dust cloth?*

Downstairs again he had to wake Wila from a deep sleep to tell her he was leaving. He showed her the panties and scolded her for dusting and destroying any possibility of recovering finger-prints.

"You wrong, Sam. I don' dus' at night," she said in a huff. "It musta been da *moke* fella."

"Sorry, Auntie," mumbled Sam. "Yeah, looks like the guy was savvy enough to sanitize the scene before he left. Auntie, is there any chance you've got an insurance description or photos of the pieces the thief stole?"

"No, Sam, I don' believe in insurance. Is a waste a money. But I migh' have a picture of me wearin' da brooch, yah."

"That would be great, Auntie. Where would I find it?"

"In da album, silly. Over der on the shelf, da las' one. Yah, dat's it."

Sam brought the album to her. Wila rearranged her bruised body to get more comfortable in the recliner and began flipping pages. Forward, then backward, one at a time until she stopped and slowly separated a four-by-six-inch photo from the page. It wasn't the clearest shot, nor the best angle. But still…

"Excellent, Auntie! This'll certainly do the trick," he said, tucking the photo into his small leather man-purse hanging from his belt.

* * * *

He parked the cab, leaving Goldie in charge, in the underground lot next door to HPD headquarters on Beretania. Next, he sought out Sergeant Pop Lione in Robbery to file a formal report on the assault and stolen items.

"Hey, Sam," said Pop, his voice upbeat and welcoming. "How you been? Didn't expect to see you again so soon." He extended his hand for a friendly shake. Gone was the annnoyed, suspicious Pop. Now he felt a professional gratitude to the ex-cop who had solved the armed robbery case at Hello Gorgeous.

"Unexpected for me too, Pop." Sam handed him his report, waited for Pop to scan it, and added, "The perp wiped down the bedroom. There aren't any insurance descriptions either." Sam displayed his iPhone photos of Auntie's injuries and asked, "Would you need to send Forensics over to compare the blood on Wila's scalp with the smear of blood on the closet door?"

Pop shook his gray head. "Not necessary. As you suspected, without fingerprints or insurance descriptions there's not much we can do."

"I'm hoping this will make a difference," Sam said. He handed over the photo of the scrimshaw ship mounted in a gold filigree brooch. "Isolated, blown-up, and distributed to all the pawn shops and jewelers in town should do the job. I'll even distribute them for you. I want to catch this *moke* who terrorizes and beats up old ladies."

"Hey, Sam, that won't be necessary," said Pop. "No need for you to do our job. By the way, the guys still talk big story about you in Homicide. You were a good cop, and obviously you're a good PI, as I found out first-hand. I know how concerned you must be, especially the lady being a family member. I'll let you know if we get any feedback on the photo."

Pleased with his progress, Sam returned to his cab. He and Goldie called it a night.

* * * *

After work two days later, Sam found a heartening message on his landline answering machine. Wila's stolen pieces had been located: three rings, a pendant, and a brooch matching the photo. He called Sergeant Lione, thanked him for acting on the case so quickly, and learned the details. A reformed one-time fence—now a small-business jeweler—had become suspicious. He convinced the would-be seller that he needed more time to evaluate the pieces and suggested that the man leave them and return the next day for payment. The *moke* hesitated and shook his head slowly.

"Just the scrimshaw piece then," suggested the jeweler, concerned that he was losing both the purchase and the apprehension of the thief.

Reluctantly, the thief agreed and hurried out. The jeweler immediately called the police. Under Pop's direction, the Robbery Division planned a trap.

The next morning Sam returned to Auntie's with the good news, but he wasn't prepared for her reaction.

Defying her injuries, Wila sprang out of her recliner with surprising agility. "Sam, you take me there. I wanna see da *moke* arrested with my own eyes. Yah." She did a little dance and swung a fist at the imaginary crook. "I make tha' bassard pay fo wha he did to me."

It took almost thirty minutes for feisty Wila to calm down enough to hear Sam out.

"Auntie, you know I love you, but you need to stay home. It would be too dangerous for you to be present when they take him into custody. But I promise you, I'll be there when the action goes down and I'll come back and report everything to you." It was a bit of a lie. He wasn't sure the police would want him there either.

At one-thirty that afternoon Sam and Goldie took up their

positions. Sam turned off the ignition and sat back to wait. Sergeant Lione had told him he could park his cab across the street and one door away to watch them make the collar—but on one condition: "As long as you don't interfere, Sam."

The jeweler and the *moke* had agreed to terms over the phone and scheduled a two o'clock meeting at the jewelry shop.

From his position Sam saw the *moke* strolling toward the jewelry shop, fifteen minutes early. He watched the thief suspiciously scan up, down, and across the street before walking boldly inside. Sam had no way of knowing what went wrong in the shop, but in just a few minutes, the *moke* burst through the front door and dashed across the street waving his hand, yelling "Taxi!"

Sam had no intention of letting him in. He instantly reached for the door-lock button, but his reflexes failed him. The *moke* flung the door open, slid into the rear seat, and slammed the door shut.

"Drive outta here quick!" he bellowed.

When Sam didn't respond quickly enough, the *moke* slipped his belt from his pants loops, flipped it over Sam's head, and with both hands pulled it tight around the cabbie's neck.

"Maybe now you'll get moving."

Protective Goldie growled, barked, and struggled, but she was secured in her harness. Choking, barely able to breathe, Sam stretched to reach the ignition key and started the engine. He imperceptibly unhooked the dog's harness from the seatbelt lock and pumped his fist. Goldie flipped around, leaped over the seat back, and landed clumsily in the *moke's* lap. The golden clamped her jaws down hard on his right wrist.

"Aaah!" he yelled and released his hold on the belt.

Sam yanked the belt away from his neck and over his head, and threw it on the passenger-side floor. Chest heaving as he caught his breath, he shifted into DRIVE and pulled away from the curb. Luckily, the street was empty. He did a U-turn and screeched to a stop directly in front of the jewelry shop just as two plainclothes detectives appeared from surrounding shop doorways. Their guns

144

were drawn. The *moke's* early arrival had taken them by surprise.

One detective pulled the rear door open.

It was all over for the stunned thief, whose wrist was still clamped firmly in Goldie's jaws. Sam clapped his hands sharply. She obediently released her grip, swiveled her body around, and climbed back into her shotgun seat.

Witnessing this drama, the astonished detectives yanked the perp out of the back seat. Lifting him up by his armpits, they set him on his feet and cuffed his wrists behind his back. As they were about to walk him to their cruiser, his unbelted cargo pants— weighted down by the rest of Wila's loot—slipped over his hips and dropped to his ankles, exposing his red polka-dot boxer undershorts.

Sam guffawed, whipped out his iPhone, and snapped two photos through the windshield. Still laughing, he turned to Goldie and handed her a Milk Bone.

"Hey, partner," he said. "Let's head over to Auntie Wila's right now. She'll get a kick out of the *moke's* final takedown."

Episode Eleven
Carnival Caper

SOPHIE KALIMALU, THE OVERWEIGHT CARD SHARK WITH MULtiple chins, sat at a table inside a flimsy tent, shuffling and reshuffling a deck. Kapiʻolani Park had been transformed into a fairground, and her little space was one of many in the Whorlly Brothers Carnival. Sophie's sleight-of-hand tactics and card tricks were too well-known among Honolulu's resident gambling trade, but a virtual magnet to the unsuspecting tourists who flocked to the carnival. But even Sophie couldn't predict the terrible hand dealt late that Saturday night.

An innocent couple, wheat farmers from Iowa, had just slunk away from her, eighty dollars poorer than when they arrived. Their game: fifteen short minutes of Shuffle and Cut for a double sawbuck a cut. Oh, they won high card twice in the first three cuts to draw them in, but it was downhill after that. They'd swallowed her come-on hook, line, and sinker and kept on betting.

Now, near eleven o'clock, as the foot traffic grew scarce, Sophie switched to the showier shuffles: springing cards from one hand to the other over an arc a foot apart, while she pitched her spiel in a booming voice.

"Hey, hon! Wanna try yer luck?…Hello, there, Handsome! Feelin' lucky tonight? How 'bout…"

Sophie's hands never stopped, but her voice trailed off

when a commotion erupted across the midway at Happy Harry's Shooting Gallery. A burly man, belly overflowing his shorts and T-shirt, had skinny Harry by the collar of his aloha shirt, yanking him upward and over the counter until the poor guy buckled to the ground out front.

"Hey, let go a me! I ain't done nothin' to you!" Harry squealed, as he was hauled to his feet.

"You're a liar and a cheat!" shouted the burly attacker. "You promised me the top pick of the prizes—that life-size stuffed penguin—if I shot a perfect hundred. Well, you saw me shoot a perfect hundred, and you handed me this lousy three-inch monkey doll worth somewhere between a dime and a quarter." He shoved Harry backward against the counter with one powerful thrust.

Harry reached behind himself and grabbed one of the loaded .22-caliber target rifles. Hoping to frighten the customer off, he fired at what he assumed was the ground. Instead, he put a live round into the huge man's left shoe.

Howling, the man's beefy fists released Harry. He raged, cursed, and threatened. Then, like a wounded animal, he turned and limped off out of sight. Harry laid the gun back on the counter and retreated behind it. Climbing onto his tall stool, he hugged his upper arms, shaking all over.

Observing this scene, Sophie grabbed the bottle of cheap whiskey she kept under the table and wriggled to her feet. In her ballooning muʻumuʻu, she waddled across the midway to Harry and offered him a drink. He took a long drag, nearly finished the bottle, and handed it back to her. She upended it and took the final swig.

Harry whimpered, "Thanks, Soph. I needed that. I thought the big bull was gonna kill me."

"Maybe you oughtta call it quits fer tonight. It's almost shuttin' down time anyway," said Sophie, as she tossed the empty bottle in the trash basket next to his tent.

"You're right, Soph." Harry packed the four target rifles and ammo into a lock-box carrying case and zippered up his tent, then trudged across the grass to his pickup parked two blocks away on Paki Avenue.

Sophie lumbered back to her shuffling and pitching.

* * * *

Sam still loved his ex-wife and absolutely adored Peggy. He treasured his visitation rights and privileges every Sunday from 10 a.m. to 10 p.m. Today he planned to take her to the Whorlly Brothers' carnival. He had informed her protective mother of their outing and was startled when Kia turned the plan into an invitation for herself as well. Sam knew his daughter yearned to have her parents together again. He secretly harbored the same hope. After all, he wasn't the same depressed, bitter, unemployed ex-cop he'd been two years ago when she initiated the divorce. It wasn't a subject they could easily discuss. For today, he'd just enjoy the small gift of her unexpected company.

He parked outside their condo and unclipped Goldie from her harness. After he punched in the intercom security code, Kia buzzed them into the building. The apartment door was already open when they stepped out of the elevator. Goldie bounded inside and Peggy flopped down on the floor to wrestle with her. A bemused Sam watched. He couldn't quite get used to his little-kid daughter now thirteen and taller than her mother. Not surprising, considering that he was six-four. Most significant, she'd inherited her mother's self-assurance and analytical skills. He still could barely wrap his head around Peggy's astonishing ability to overcome two dangerous bank robbers.

Kia called from the kitchen: "I was thinking of packing sandwiches so we can make a whole day of it."

"Phooey!" Peggy blurted out.

"What's wrong with Mom making sandwiches?" Sam asked, not wanting to start an argument.

Still hugging Goldie, Peggy made a face. "I know what she'll do. She'll make 'em with tofu and kale. Yuck! I want hotdogs and chili and cotton candy."

Kia came into the living room laughing. "It's okay. Maybe

148

I'd like a chili dog and garlic fries too. I'm not all ogre."

"Cool, Mom!" Peggy said.

The carnival turned out to be a small traveling operation from the Mainland: a Ferris wheel, kiddy rides, and sporty games requiring a range of skills. Larger tents touted games of chance, a fortune teller, a puppet show, and Hawai'i-made crafts. Delicious aromas wafted from the culinary booths: from sizzling dogs and burgers to spring rolls and Spam *musubi*. A twelve-piece band, set up in the park's orchestra shell, continually played Hawai'ian melodies. Hula dancers from a local teen *hui* performed on the stage in front of the band.

Peggy pulled her parents over to the midway. She had won a stuffed dolphin at the hoop toss and wanted to try her luck at a wheel where a dollar-a-spin guaranteed you a prize. While she waited her turn, Sam, already bored and restless, scanned the crowd. He noticed yellow crime scene tape wrapped around a closed tent. He also saw a familiar face there. "Be right back," he said, and hobbled over.

"Hey, brah, what's going on here?"

Detective Sergeant Danny Oshiro stared at him. "Hi, Sam. I didn't think you were into carnivals."

"Not usually, but I'm here with Peggy and Kia just for the fun of it. I take it this is a crime scene."

"Sure is. Early this morning we found Happy Harry's body in one of the parking lots, next to a pickup truck—at least we're pretty sure it's his. Blunt force trauma to the head. We're guessing the killer grabbed him by the hair and slammed his head against the driver's-side door. We found target rifles and ammo locked away in the pickup cab, plus a few carny signs in the truck bed for Happy Harry's Shooting Gallery. That's what led us over here, but we're at a dead end right now. No witnesses."

"I always wondered how you can have a live shooting gallery with so many people milling around," said Sam. "It doesn't seem safe to me."

"It's not idiot-proof," replied Danny. "But a booth fitted

out with one-inch armor plate and a couple inches of cotton batting on the backdrop and side wings pretty much contains it. An intentional shortage of gunpowder affects velocity, impact, and even accuracy. Especially accuracy," he added, eyebrows raised with a knowing look.

"Well, thanks for the lesson. I'd better get back to my family before I get in trouble. Good luck with the case."

"Thanks. Take care, Sam."

Sam turned and took a few ski-walk steps when he heard "Pssst! Pssst!" He spotted Sophie, his favorite old-time snitch, sitting in her tent with a customer. The sullen-faced man, an obvious loser, rose and left. She motioned for Sam to enter. He squeezed in beside her.

"Take a load off, Copper," she said. "I wont bite ya."

Sam grinned. "Howzit going, Sophie?" he asked, sitting down on the adjacent folding chair. "Today I'm here for fun with my family, not information from you."

Sophie nodded, her several chins bobbing. "I'm good. I know you ain't a copper no more, but you once told me I wuz still yer snitch, an' anyways I got somethin' to say to you." Her blue eyes filled with tears before she was able to continue. "I heard wha' happened to poor Harry over der. It was bad business. He wuz in a fight las' nigh' and I know who with—at least wha' he looked like. Yah."

"The homicide detectives are still looking around in his tent," Sam said. "Why don't you go across and tell *them* what you know?"

"I don' trus' any coppers like I trus' you. They always wanna arrest me fer cheatin' an' all. Maybe I do, but that ain't no reason to bust me, is it?"

"I value your high-quality intel, Sophie, and I appreciate you, especially now that I have my PI license. To the police you're operating outside the law. Maybe I bend it a little too. So tell me what happened here last night."

Sophie described the pissed-off brawny customer, and gave

Sam a pretty good blow-by-blow of the argument and manhandling that went down the night before.

Sam sensed that Sophie had some feelings for Harry. "Were you and Harry close?" he asked.

"We wuz not lovers, if that's what ya mean. Jus' frens. He brung a bottle and a movie over to my place once a week. That's all. Yah."

"When he had the fight in his booth, do you think the bullet actually hit the customer's shoe?" Sam asked.

"The way that guy limped, it's a sure thing—right through the leatha shoe, I betcha. Harry closed up his booth and went home a few minutes after."

"Thanks, Sophie." Sam slipped a twenty-dollar bill under her water bottle, then straightened up with Cane and Able.

"This wuz s'posed to be a freebee from me, Copper. I see you still usin' them giant chopsticks to get around, yah."

"I always appreciate your help, Sophie. As for the chopsticks, they're here forever. Take care now, girl."

Sam plodded across the midway once more to talk with Danny, who was currently interviewing a fortune teller from an adjacent booth. He waited until they were finished. "Hey, Danny—"

"I thought you went back to your family," interrupted the detective in a grumpy, impatient voice.

"If you're nice to me, I can make your whole day. I've got a description of the man you're looking for."

"Sorry, Sam, this case is getting to me. Nobody saw or heard a thing. At least that's what they're telling me. Or rather not telling me. What's with this carnival bunch, anyway? Okay, what've *you* got for me?"

"There apparently was an altercation last night at Happy Harry's Shooting Gallery," Sam related precisely what Sophie had described.

"Wait!" said Danny. "We estimated the stiff to weigh just under one-fifty. You're saying this customer pulled him over the top like a sack of potatoes?"

"My informant said he was a big mother."

"Sam, where in hell are you getting all this, and is it reliable?"

"From one of my former snitches. She thinks of me as a friend too. She was an eyewitness to the fight, and she's already heard through the grapevine about the body in the parking lot. From the way she talked to me about Harry, past tense, I think she's pretty sure it's him. She's very reliable, Danny—always since I've known her, but she won't talk to any cops now. Says I'm the only one she trusts. She says she can ID the big guy in the fight, and I think I can persuade her to testify. Because of the guy's wounded foot, any blood the crime scene unit finds could belong to *either* the victim or the perp."

"I'm afraid your snitch is going to have to talk to me whether she wants to or not."

"You can try. Be patient with her, Danny. She's in the tent directly across from the shooting gallery."

"The big woman?"

"Yeah. Her name is Sophie Kalimalu. She's a shuffle-and-cut scammer. Her usual haunt is the Bottleneck Bar and Grille in Waikīkī. Be careful with her. I still need her as an intel source and she's fragile right now. At least emotionally."

Popping out of the crowd, Peggy, Kia, and Goldie showed up at the shooting gallery. "Daddy, what's taking you so long?" Peggy asked, sounding as bossy as her lawyer mother. She held Goldie by the leash, but not tightly enough. The dog lunged forward, leash and all, and scooted under the police tape to a UH Rainbow Warriors cap lying on the ground next to the gun counter. Snatching it up in her teeth, she bounded back to Sam and laid it at his feet.

"Hey, you crazy dog!" shouted Danny. "You're contaminating my crime scene." Goldie scurried to safety behind her master. "Sam, I shouldn't have to tell you, this is a people park, not a dog park. Get your mutt out of here." He walked across the midway to interview Sophie.

Sam lost his cool. Unaccustomed to being chewed out by

152

his detective friend, especially in public, he forgot about the cap on the ground and half-stumbled a few yards away. Kia scowled at her daughter. Peggy's cheeks turned red. She stooped down to grab Goldie's leash, tightened her grip on it, and hurried after her father. But she was determined to redeem herself. "Daddy, what about the cap Goldie found?"

Sam suddenly realized he'd forgotten all about it. He pivoted to look where it had been lying. It was gone. He spotted a hulking man in a Rainbow Warriors cap limping down the midway away from them.

A scream emerged from Sophie's tent. "Dat's him!" she cried. Glaring at Danny, she yelled, "You da copper, you get tha' murderin' son-of-a-bitch."

Danny struggled to squeeze past her. "Stop! Police!" he yelled as soon as he caught sight of the bruiser. "Stop! Police!" The man lurched off between the tents and out of sight. Danny broke into a run, tripped over a tent peg, and fell to the ground.

Sam reached down and unclipped Goldie's leash, looked her straight in her alert eyes, and pumped his left fist, opening and closing his fingers. The retriever took off like she was shot from a cannon, down the midway to the area between the tents where the bruiser was last seen, then veered right, and dropped out of sight in the escapee's direction.

While Danny scrambled to his feet, Sam maneuvered between the tents. Just beyond the last kiddy ride he spotted the bruiser headed across the grass toward Paki Avenue, with Goldie galloping some twenty yards behind and closing fast.

Sam's heart skipped a beat. The traffic on Paki was clogged with fairgoers looking for parking spaces. If the perp darted between cars, Goldie would follow and likely be killed.

A split second later, he could breathe again. Still on the grass in the park, Goldie flew through the air, a missile landing on the back of the huge man's knees. The bruiser managed a string of stumbles and finally tripped himself in a hard fall on his face. Goldie caught up with him, and sank her teeth into his right ankle. The man howled and swatted at her with his right hand, but couldn't reach her. Next, he tried to kick her with his sore foot and that didn't work either. Lying flat on his stomach left him with no alternative but surrender.

Danny bolted forward from behind the Ferris wheel, his sinewy body recovered and not the least bit stressed as he closed in. Arriving on the scene, he immediately slapped plastic restraints on the now-docile perp.

Almost comically, the bruiser kept hollering commands like "No" and "Free" to Goldie, but she continued to grip his ankle. Sam arrived and clapped his hands loud enough for Goldie to release her grip, the way he'd trained her.

Sam sensed that the sergeant was about to ask him for help lifting the perp to his feet. "Hang on a minute, Danny, I need to check something out." He noticed that the bruiser's large, wide feet were in sandals, not leather shoes like Sophie had described. Poking out of the open-toed left-foot sandal was a gauze bandage wrapped around the toes, with a small smear of blood alongside the pinkie. *That's where Harry's bullet must have grazed the guy's foot,* Sam surmised. *Minimal injury, which is why he was able to come back to the carnival today.*

Sam and Danny hoisted the brawny man to his feet, with hands cuffed behind him. In a loud, firm voice Danny Mirandized him, then turned him over to the two officers waiting to transport him to headquarters.

"Hey Danny," Sam said, as Goldie nuzzled up against his leg. "The three of us make a pretty good team."

"Yeah, though I'm embarrassed to admit it. Thanks, Sam, one more time." The two men shook hands.

"You too, girl." He reached down to stroke Goldie's head. She gave his hand a forgiving lick.

"Our perp will be tried and convicted of second-degree murder and probably get fifteen years of prison time," said Danny. "That is, if some fancy-pants lawyer doesn't come up with a defense to get him less time."

Go figure, thought Sam. *If only Harry hadn't been such a penny-pincher. If he hadn't cheated the perp out of the stuffed penguin, he would still be alive and his customer would have gone home happy.*

§

Episode Twelve
The Snake Lady

QUACK, QUACK, QUACK. THE COMIC RING TONE BLASTED from the dashboard on Sam's smart phone. Peggy had slyly substituted it for his normal bugle-reveille tone. Every time it quacked, Goldie barked, wondering where the duck was. They were zipping back to town on Nimitz Highway from Pier 38, where they'd dropped off a couple for lunch at Uncle's Seafood Restaurant.

Sam activated the no-hands call. "That you, Auntie Momi? Howzit? You need a ride? What's the story with your old Chevy?.... I guess we all gotta get old sometime....No, not you, your car. I'll pick you up in ten minutes. Yah."

On a quiet street in Kalihi, he pulled up in front of a canary-yellow wood-frame house. Momi Kela waved from her rocking chair. She padded down the walk in her teal-blue mu'umu'u sprinkled with red hibiscus blooms. Charging through the gate to the street, she opened the cab door and plopped down into the back seat.

Goldie strained so hard to greet Auntie that Sam had to release the harness, so she could turn around. Momi leaned forward for a slobbering of glad-to-see-you licks.

"Okay, okay! So where to, Auntie? Can't stay here all day. We two got a living to make."

"I go see Snake Lady today." Momi fumbled around in her purse for a slip of paper holding the address. "Ah, here it is. 203 Kapiolohi Street."

"Snake Lady? What's that all about, Auntie?"

"*Kilo nānā lima*, my fortune teller. Why you ask?"

"No reason except that not everyone has a name like Snake Lady." Sam turned the cab toward the Kalihi address less than a mile away.

"I'm the only one who call her that. She keep a snake in da house, a python, I think. He a pretty boy, nice pet. She call him Heki. *Naheka* is Hawai'ian for snake. He slither all over da place, but he never bother da clients. Last time I got to watch her feed 'im. He only need a live mouse once a week."

"What? Auntie, you've gotta be kidding. Snakes are illegal in Hawai'i. How big is this one anyway?"

"'Bout so." In the rear-view mirror Sam saw that she had stretched her arms in ruffled sleeves as far as they would go. "Jeez! Three feet. That's a granddaddy. You sure you want to go see the Snake Lady?"

"Yah, I go all the time. I no scaredy-cat."

Sam drew up to the address, a white clapboard house set back about fifteen feet in a small but well-tended yard next door to a vacant lot. "Maybe I should wait for you, Auntie."

"Oh, no, Sam, dear. She tell my fortune, den we *talk story*. Hour, hour and half. I call you when I done."

Sam waited out front until he saw Auntie Momi knock on the door, then walk right in. Before he could shift into DRIVE, she burst back out, screaming and wildly waving her hands. Sam shut off the engine, put the shift gear in PARK, and set the emergency brake. Grabbing Cane and Able, he slid out of the cab and ski-walked to the lanai.

"What's wrong, Auntie?"

"Da Snake Lady. She on da floor like a dead chicken. Her neck's wrung all funny-like."

"Now, Auntie, calm down! You go wait in the cab with

Goldie. There's bottled water in the seat pocket and a Thermos full of hot tea. You gonna be okay?"

"No. Yah. I guess." Her throaty voice trembled.

Sam watched as she hastily climbed into the back seat, then he turned and entered the tiny foyer. The room immediately on the left was the parlor, the fortune teller's inner sanctum, where she set the mood, feeding the hopes and dreams of her clients. An aura of make-believe surrounded him. The windows were draped in purple velvet. A Tiffany-type fixture in multicolored glass hung low from the ceiling. Sam looked about uneasily. He hated snakes. Was he going to confront a three-foot python in the shadows? So far, no.

He found the Snake Lady on the thick oriental rug next to an overturned gate-leg table. Her large crystal ball had rolled to the nearest wall—not even cracked. He saw no sign of the snake, but his eyes darted about every few seconds to be absolutely sure. The deceased was a heavyset local woman of sixty-plus with no obvious wounds or sign of blood. She wore gold hoop earrings and a fringed shawl studded with gold bangles over a long black dress. An aqua turban covered her head, fixed in front by a rhinestone ruby, but not completely hiding her salt-and-pepper hair. Sam got a sick feeling in his gut. Auntie Momi was right. The head was misaligned, slightly askew and out of whack from the rest of the body. Patterned red marks formed a two-inch band around the bare neck with sharply outlined edges. His first impression was that the woman had been strangled by her own python. *But why would an experienced snake handler allow this to happen? Especially when it's her pet,* he thought. His eyes scanned the room once more, then the four adjoining rooms. In the last one he found a fifty-gallon aquarium tank with the cover off. No snake.

Returning to the cab, Sam saw that his auntie had recovered from the shock. He found her chatting away through the cab's rolled-down rear window with a tall, strapping *haole* woman.

"Sam," Momi said, her dark eyes sparkling with importance. "Dis lady lives next door."

Now there's a grapevine starter if I ever saw one, he thought. In the front seat Goldie was yelping and bouncing up and down. Sam knew what that meant. He released the harness, clipped on her leash, and took her for her call to nature—and her chance to sniff the tree trunks, the canine communications network.

Sam had some communicating to do as well. He punched in Sergeant Oshiro. "Hey, Danny, I'm here in Kalihi on Kapiolohi Street. I've got a dead body for you. Looks like strangulation, but of course I can't tell by what. No, I haven't messed up your crime scene. You know me better than that." Sam held up the slip of paper Momi had given him and read the address aloud. "Okay! I'll wait for you....Of course I'll steer clear of the crime scene. You have my word."

By the time he returned to the cab with Goldie, Auntie Momi and the next-door neighbor had retreated to her lanai, and were chatting nonstop like lifelong buddies. They had secured front-row rattan seats to a police investigation! Crossing the lawn, Sam approached them.

"Hello, ma'am, I'm a private investigator." He flashed his credentials. "The police are on their way."

The woman stood as he came near.

"And your name is?" Sam asked.

"Valerie Button."

With hands on her hips, Valerie looked to be about forty, busty and self-assured, with a fair-skinned freckled face. She wore neatly pressed jeans and a sleeveless shirt in the trendy asymmetrical style.

"Valerie, do you know the names of the people next door?"

"Maile Kenoi," she said. "Nobody else. She's lived there alone at least twenty years that I remember. Her husband died long ago. Nice lady. My friend, actually, but a little strange—her pet and all that fortune-telling and stuff."

"Any regular male or female callers?" asked Sam, jotting down a few notes in his small spiral pad. "Maybe a love interest?"

"The only man I ever see come calling is that creepy grandson of hers, Kimo Kenoi." Valerie shuddered saying his name.

"Did she go out much?"

"Only for shopping and back. She liked the TV and her magazines mostly."

"What about her clients? They're all female?"

"Who else goes to a fortune teller?" asked Valerie, adding a wise-ass tinge to her voice.

"She ever mention any dissatisfied clients?"

"Nothing major. Maybe a detail she didn't get right, or a husband trying to squash his wife's visits. We *talked story* all the time, but she never mentioned anyone who was a problem. Usually, she was upbeat, sending them away with something good to hope for. She always did most of the talking."

"Any children or siblings that you know of to be notified?" asked Sam.

"Nope, just the grandson."

"Do you know how to get in touch with him?"

"I think I've got an emergency number somewhere that Maile gave me a while back. I'll look." Valerie strode inside, letting the screen door bang.

"Bring it here when you find it, ma'am, please," Sam called after her.

Goldie suddenly bolted forward with such strength that Sam lost his hold on the leash. She galloped deep into the empty lot on the opposite side of Maile's house and nearly disappeared among the shaggy grasses and weeds. Sam heard frantic barking and was about to give chase before she could get too far away.

Just then the police cruiser pulled up, siren blaring. Sam waved Danny down and pointed out the house. While Danny went inside, Sam pursued the frantic barks—and lurched to a stop. Goldie was dashing back and forth, the attached leash flopping. And then he saw why. An enormous snake lay coiled up, sunning itself on top of a large flat rock. It seemed oblivious to the commotion as long as Goldie kept her distance, but she raised her head as Sam got nearer.

160

"Goldie, no!" he yelled. "Come!"

Reluctantly, she obeyed.

"Sit!" She sat down beside his left leg while he grabbed the leash and wound the loop tightly around his fist. Sam again pulled out his smart phone and pointed it at the snake for a few snapshots. Coming face to face with the huge creature set his stomach churning. But he had to admit a certain fascination with Mother Nature's artistry: gold and beige irregular shapes against a black background. The long head had black and gold horizontal stripes with a dash of white underneath. His first impulse was to dial the authorities. But he stopped himself. Danny would never forgive him for overstepping his bounds. Sam knew that protocol meant a lot to the detective. *My friend's Japanese ancestry might have something to do with it,* he thought.

He walked Goldie back to the cab and harnessed her, much to the dog's disappointment. She'd seen Auntie on the lanai next door and wanted to be included in the socializing. But Sam had more important things to think about. *It's illegal to keep a snake in Hawai'i. I wonder how she managed to smuggle one in—especially a three-foot python. At least that's what Auntie says it is.*

Another five minutes and Danny came through Maile's front door with a handkerchief held over his mouth and nose. "Whew. By the smell of things, I'd say she's been dead a few days, and this heat sure doesn't help matters any either."

"At least a couple of days," Sam said. "And by the way, Danny, there's something else. The lady was a fortune teller and owned a pet snake, possibly a python. It's sunning itself in the vacant lot next door, for the moment, anyway. The killer may have let it out."

Danny groaned. "Oh for crissake. Not another damn reptile. No matter how hard we try, the black market thrives. Take me there."

Approaching the rock, but keeping their distance, Sam didn't expect Danny's reaction: "That's one helluva beautiful animal." He took out his cell and dialed the PEST HOTLINE at the Hawai'i Department of Agriculture Plant Quarantine Branch. While they waited for the inspector to arrive, they discussed the victim's body.

"Hey, Sam. The awkward head position—what do you think it means?"

"Well, now that I've had a chance to think about it, I'm convinced that this is a homicide. I don't see a live wrap-around snake snapping a person's neck. I'm no expert, of course, but I would think snake strangulation is a slow and steady crushing, finally choking off the air supply, muscle by muscle, snake versus woman. I can't envision a quick snapping move here. The patterned markings on the neck do resemble those of the python on the rock. There's just one problem with those markings."

"What's that?" asked Danny.

"The edges of the snake patterns are outlined, forming a definite band around the woman's neck. It seems to me that a cross-section of the snake's body is round and wouldn't leave an accented edge like that. I'm thinking that a python's snake skin was used to strangle the poor woman. When she put up a struggle, the killer resorted to a sharp, yanking stroke, which broke her neck."

"And blame it all on the snake," Danny said. "Except where does anyone get hold of a python skin in Hawai'i?"

"Where does anyone get anything these days?" posed Sam.

"The Internet, of course," Danny replied. "But that's illegal too—trafficking in reptile skins."

As they were talking, the state Ag Department truck rolled up. A couple of handshakes and they learned details from the inspector. "It's a ball python, a well-fed, full-grown male. They're constrictors, but docile, nonpoisonous, and make good pets." After Danny explained that the owner was dead, the inspector said he'd take charge of the python. He fetched a pole from his truck, gently lifted Heki up, and carried it to a containment bin. "Unfortunately," he explained, "we're holding dozens of snakes and other illegal reptiles smuggled in. We'll be shipping them to the Mainland to various reptile farms. The penalty for owning one in Hawai'i is up to three years in prison and a $200,000 fine. But we have an amnesty plan now. Bring it to us, and we'll accept it, no questions asked, no penalties."

After the inspector left, Sam and Danny resumed their speculation on motives. Pushing his sunglasses up into his curly black hair that now had a few rogue gray hairs peeking out, Sam was on a roll. "Here we have a widow, living alone in the same home for twenty years. I think we can assume that love, passion, hate, and revenge are a little far-fetched. As for envy or money, the house is quite modest and the neighborhood as well, so unless she's got cash socked away or the neighborhood is about to appreciate significantly, envy and money aren't likely motives either."

"Hey, buddy, you're making too many assumptions," Danny said, irked by the pontificating. "My next move is to interview the grandson. He might be the one who'd benefit most from Mrs. Kenoi's death. "You can join me if you want to."

Sam wanted to. The following day, he and Danny arrived separately to meet with Kimo in front of Mrs. Kenoi's house. Not inside. Both front and back doors were blocked with yellow crime-scene tape.

Arriving on a blue moped, Kimo Kenoi was a large, polite young man with a kind face and troubled expression. "My granny didn't deserve this. She was a good soul."

"We're sorry for your loss," Danny said. "This is a routine question, Kimo, but I have to ask. Where were you three days ago in the late afternoon?"

"I get it, Detective. I was at my after-school job at Ace Hardware on Wai'alae. You can check. I'm a senior at Kalani High." He dug his fists into the pockets of his baggy shorts.

"Thank you," Danny said. "Did Mrs. Kenoi own the vacant lot next door?"

"No. Her neighbor Valerie Button owns it, plus a few other lots around here."

"How do you know that?" asked Sam.

"She bragged about them," replied Kimo. "Called them her

insurance policy."

"Were Valerie and your granny friends?" Sam asked.

"Used to be. My *tutu* didn't trust her anymore. A few weeks ago Mrs. Button invited me in for a beer. She wanted to buy Granny's house and asked me to persuade Granny to sell it to her. I admit I tried. I thought Granny might make a nice profit, but she loved her house and didn't want any part of such a deal. Mrs. Button got kinda angry when I reported back. She said something really weird."

"Like what?" asked Sam.

"It was more a question: '*You'd sell it to me if it was yours, wouldn't you?*' I nearly flipped. I got outta there fast." He looked at his Timex watch; the face showed a surfer catching a wave. "Sorry, but I gotta go. I'm late for work." Kimo turned to leave, but wheeled back around. "I almost forgot. When I went to ID Granny's body I noticed that her favorite ring was gone."

"Was it important?" asked Danny.

"Yeah, real important. To me too." Tears welled up in Kimo's eyes. "I gave it to her for her birthday. It's really cool. The stone is quartz, a large oval in earthy reds and browns, and a sterling-silver snake, all hand-made, with the head on top of the stone and the tail curled around the bottom. I got it in Chinatown. It cost me a week's salary, but she loved it. She called it her Heki ring."

Sam again whipped out his spiral pad. Impressed with Kimo's articulate description, he took careful notes. Danny thanked the young man, and they watched him ride off on his moped.

* * * *

Two days later, while Goldie visited Peggy and her mom, Sam dug into his favorite meal, oxtail soup and a meatloaf sandwich at Zippy's. His smart phone quacked. A few customers turned their heads and giggled. It was Danny reporting in.

"So it was the grandson after all," Sam concluded.

"No, Sam. Now we're looking at the neighbor lady. I was frustrated. The case was going nowhere until I read Sunday's paper, the financial pages on local real estate activity. One of the big retailers wants to put up a local market in Mrs. Kenoi's neighborhood. They're applying for a variance as we speak. They're planning to buy up all the surrounding properties. Apparently, Valerie got wind of it weeks ago. The company is prepared to pay big bucks to all owners. She wanted Mrs. Kenoi's house badly to make a killing—sorry, bad choice of words." Danny paused a moment to collect his thoughts. "Anyway, I got suspicious. Especially coupled with what Kimo told us. There's our motive, Sam. But we're not done. We don't have—"

"—the murder weapon," Sam burst in. "So what's next?"

"I just got a search warrant for Valerie's house. Two officers are headed there with it right now. I'm meeting them there. Want to join us?"

Sam could hardly contain himself. "You bet." He paid his bill and got his lunch packed in takeout containers. Fifteen minutes later he pulled up to the curb to find Valerie on the lawn, arguing with Danny.

"This is outrageous, Detective, a blatant invasion of my privacy," she shouted, waving the search warrant in front of his face.

It was all for show; the two police officers were already inside. After a meticulous search, with Danny and Sam waiting in the front hall, an officer called out, "Got something! Better come on up."

Danny took the stairs two at a time. When Sam finally arrived in the back bedroom, one officer had just set a large hat box on the bed. The cover was off.

Danny reported, "We found this stashed in the drop ceiling." Above them the police had removed several ceiling tiles, showing that plenty of space was available for the box. Tension mounted as they all peered inside. There lay a three-foot-long snake skin.

Valerie stood in the doorway, filling it with her imposing presence. "How dare you go snooping in my personal possessions? I've never seen that thing in my life! The murderer must have planted it there. The grandson, I'll bet."

As she angrily crossed her bare arms over her chest, Sam's

gaze landed on her left hand. Exposed on her third finger, gleaming in the sunlight, was a multicolored ring with an oval stone and silver snake, exactly as Kimo had described it. The fortune teller's Heki ring. Valerie followed Sam's gaze and snapped, "So I stole the ring. So what? She had no more use for it. But that doesn't mean I killed her."

Silence reigned as four pairs of accusing eyes bore into her.

When Valerie saw that no one was buying her protest, she broke down and confessed. "The big real estate deal would've been my retirement. That fortune teller witch was going to mess up the whole deal."

Outside, as the police cruiser carried the cuffed Valerie away, Sam turned to Danny. "Well, you've got one more collar under your belt. Congratulations." But he spoke the words with a lack of genuine feeling.

"What's wrong, Sam?" asked Danny, sensing the change in mood.

"I believed the woman. But she was a cool, lying customer. Maybe I'm too naive."

Danny laughed. "Not you, Sam. Thanks for everything, good buddy. Gotta run now."

* * * *

But questions remained about the murder weapon, and HPD Forensics revealed the startling truth. Valerie had not purchased the snake skin off the Internet or from any other commercial source. Heki, the pet python, had shed it, as snakes routinely do. Mrs. Kenoi had tossed the shed skin in her garbage can. Valerie retrieved it, waiting patiently for weeks to execute the plan that was supposed to secure her financial future.

§

Close Encounters

THE NAHOE FAMILY SPENT A SUNDAY AFTERNOON VISITING Auntie Wila. Sam had worried that she might be suffering from severe anxiety after her traumatic encounter with the second-story *moke*. Not at all. They found Auntie lounging in her recliner. Even though several weeks had passed, she crowed with delight upon seeing them. The *Star-Advertiser* article had made her a neighborhood celebrity. Her head wound had healed just fine, and the police had returned all her jewelry. To anyone who would listen she bragged about "my wonderful nephew."

As the family emerged from Auntie's house, a sudden tropical storm hit, a downpour bursting from the blackened sky, soaking all four of them to the skin. A brisk wind brought with it a chill as they hurried to the Checker Cab. Sam fished out a roll of paper towels that he kept under the console between the front seats, so they could at least dry their hands and faces. Before anyone realized it, Goldie's fur was squeegeeing rainwater into the upholstery of her shotgun seat.

"Forget about the restaurant," said Kia, wishing she'd worn an old cotton shirt instead of her best silk blouse. "We can't go to Assaggio's like this. Let's just go home."

"But what about dinner?" wailed Peggy. "I had my heart set on fettucini Alfredo, and now we'll prob'ly get PB&J sandwiches.

167

Phooey!"

"Maybe I could whip up something a little better," said her mother.

"Oh, sure, Mom. Most of our suppers come out of a box. And I haven't ever had a frozen one that tastes as good as the picture looks on the package."

Kia broke into a rueful smile. She couldn't deny it. Cooking was a pain in the butt. She'd take the courtroom over the kitchen any day.

"Or," said Sam, "we could send out for pizza, and let the delivery boy get wet."

"All right! Pizza, pizza!" trilled Peggy.

Sam turned over the engine and headed for the apartment. Ever since their carnival outing, the family had spent more and more Sundays together, despite the fact that this was supposed to be exclusive time for dad and daughter. But Sam didn't mind; he'd remarry Kia at the drop of his peaked cabbie cap. She still insisted that they abide by the divorce agreement, but lately it was also her idea to join in on their Sundays, giving Sam a shred of hope. But only a shred. Kia still kept him at arm's length, even though she admitted she enjoyed his company. But no hugs, no kisses.

The moment they entered the Kanunu Street apartment, Goldie charged into the kitchen, where she indulged in every wet dog's favorite activity: shaking herself mightily, plumed tail waving, spraying rainwater over the tile floor and all the base cabinets. Peggy giggled. "What a good dog. You didn't go for the velvet couch in the living room." Even Kia had to laugh. She grabbed bath towels from the hall linen closet and handed then to Sam. "For you and Goldie—her first, of course."

Then she and Peggy disappeared to change, leaving Sam standing alone in the kitchen. He rubbed his partner down vigorously. Goldie didn't mind the manhandling one bit, as long as somebody nice was doing something to her or for her.

Mopping himself off the best he could, Sam decided to leave and started for the front hall. He had one hand already on the doorknob to the corridor when the master bedroom door burst open. Kia appeared in a short, loosely tied, dressing gown. She handed him a terry-cloth robe.

"Sorry I left you stranded," she said.

"I'll never get one of your robes around me," said Sam.

A rare flush tinged her tawny cheeks. "Actually, it's yours. You left it behind. I couldn't part with it because it's so warm and cuddly, the way you used to be."

His eyes flicked over her well-shaped, plump knees. "I could be that way again, honest."

"We'll see," she responded, darting back to the bedroom. "I'll call in the pizza order. One extra-large, half mushroom half pepperoni. Okay?" she asked from the doorway.

"Great!"

Sam pulled off his cold, clammy polo shirt, threw on the robe, and hastily climbed out of his trousers and briefs. He dried himself thoroughly with the second bath towel, wrapped himself into the robe, and dropped the wet clothes in the kitchen sink.

Peggy wandered in from her room. Her luxurious, un-braided damp hair fell around her shoulders. Sam realized she was getting more beautiful and looking more like her mother every day.

"The pizza will be delivered in half an hour," said Kia, appearing in the kitchen once more, this time dressed in a tank top and wrap-around skirt. "I'm throwing all the wet things in the dryer." She laid a twenty-dollar bill on the table. "Peggy, here's the money for the delivery boy."

They sat around the table awaiting the arrival of supper. Sam felt self-conscious and ridiculous in his robe that wouldn't stay completely shut, especially at the knees. The dryer chugged and rotated with an occasional clunk and thud. When the doorbell finally rang, Peggy snatched the bill and opened the door. A youth in a windbreaker sodden with raindrops held out the warm box and receipt. "Thank you, keep the change," she said, and shut the door.

No sooner had Peggy placed the pizza box on the table when they heard a ruckus in the corridor and a young voice shouting, "Cut it out! Help! My wallet!" Sam reached the door first and swung it open to see the delivery boy in front of the elevator, trying to fight off a short, obese man in a biker jacket and jeans trying to wrestle him to the floor. The insulated pizza pouch lay on the floor next to them.

"Hey! Break it up!" yelled Sam, as Goldie squeezed through the doorway past him.

The fat man threw one last punch to the jaw that stunned the delivery boy and knocked him to the floor. The culprit was about to run for the fire stairs, but he got greedy. Or hungry. He grabbed the insulated pouch off the floor, then chugged down the hall for the fire stairs. The pouch contained a second pie—for delivery to another apartment—and the flap wasn't fastened.

Goldie looked back at Sam and saw him pump his left fist while leaning his right hand on Cane. She squeezed through the slowly closing air-cushioned door and gave chase. The thief was halfway down the first flight when the pouch flap popped wide open. The pizza box slid out and landed on the stairs just behind the fleeing thief. As Goldie padded down the stairs in pursuit, she bumped into the box. The cover sprang open. A pizza loaded "with everything" lay in front of her. She braked to a halt. The aroma got the better of her. She sniffed and tried to chomp into the crust, but the pizza pie flopped ahead, down one more stair with each chomp. Determined to capture the elusive pie, she jumped aboard and rode the box, pizza-boarding downward the last half-flight.

The thief heard the commotion behind him and looked over his left shoulder—so startled seeing the large dog and pizza flying at him that he tripped. "Aaaah!" he roared as he came crashing down, landing on his belly at the bottom of the stairs. The run-away pizza arrived next, just before Goldie, spreading loose cheese, pepperoni, and anchovies all over the thief. Goldie landed squarely across his lower back, cushioned by the thief pumping out his breath. He remained helpless for a minute or two. Still atop

170

him, she lapped up the blobs of pizza smearing the thief's clothes. In the struggle to get away from her, he wriggled his shoulders right and left until his flabby body threw her against the stairwell wall. Goldie struck her head hard enough to see a few stars. Only a moment later, she recovered and tried to resume her pursuit, but by then the thief had already wobbled to his feet and headed through the fire door to the lobby. Goldie was trapped at the bottom of the stairs.

Meanwhile, Sam had taken the elevator. He arrived in the lobby just as the thief burst through the door. The ex-cop stood between the perp and the front door. Sam flipped Able over and caught the thief's left ankle in the handle as he passed him. The thief fell to the floor. Sam dropped both his canes and tried to wrestle him into submission, but the perp managed to throw a punch to Sam's left eye. Seconds later, the ex-cop subdued him with a powerful wallop to the flabby stomach. Spasming in pain, the thief rolled onto his belly. The wallet he had stolen from the delivery boy and stuck in his belt now lay just inches out of his reach. Sam picked it up, struggled to his feet, and placed a bare foot in the small of the guy's back. As he stood there, he re-tightened the blue terry robe around his waist and glanced around the lobby, quite aware—*it's not exactly the outfit for detective work.*

"Get off me, you interfering gorilla," the thief yelled. "You're twice my size."

"And what did you do to that delivery boy upstairs?" said Sam.

A beleaguered grunt was the only response.

Peggy emerged from the elevator. "Mom called 9-1-1. We were worried about you, Daddy. They'll be here as soon as they can."

"Good, Peggs," said Sam. "Now hand me Cane and Able. By the way, where's Goldie?" He turned his head. "Goldie! Goldie!"

In response, several shrill barks resounded from the other side of the fire door. Peggy rushed to open it for her. Goldie stood there with her tail wagging and her nose still covered with the pizza mess, but she had had her fill by now.

About ten minutes later, two plainclothes officers from the Robbery squad arrived and took charge of the perpetrator. "Are you the victim?" asked one officer. "You sure are gonna get one hell of a shiner with that eye." He slipped a tie-wrap restraint over the thief's wrists.

"Yeah, he got one lucky punch in," replied Sam. "But no, the vic is a young kid, and he's up in my ex-wife's apartment on the third floor, 307. He had just delivered our pizza when this low-life jumped him and stole his wallet."

"So we'll be adding assault and battery to the robbery charge. Say, aren't you on the job? Homicide, isn't it?"

"I was, but now I'm retired, medically."

"How about we go up and meet with this victim?" asked one officer.

Sam pointed toward the elevator and everyone, including Goldie, squeezed in and rode up two stories. The second officer held the perp, cuffed behind his back, in the hall and Mirandized him while the rest of them entered the apartment. The delivery boy was sitting on the couch with Kia holding a cold pack to his jaw. The officer interviewed the boy and obtained both an identification of the thief and the boy's stolen property. In a quavering voice, the youth said, "I never got to make my second delivery! I have to call my boss. He'll be pissed!"

The officer kindly said, "It's not your fault, son, you're the victim here. We'll call your boss. He'll understand."

The delivery boy agreed to press charges first thing in the morning. Sam also agreed to be a witness to the petty theft and assault and battery charges.

Kia hadn't noticed the swelling in Sam's eye until after the boy and the officers had left with their prisoner. "Oh, you poor dear, you're swelling up. It's turning all red. I'll bet it hurts like the dickens. I'll get you a cold pack." She cooed as if talking to a child, and Sam loved it. He sank gratefully into a wing chair. The cold pack she'd used for the delivery boy sat on the coffee table, getting warm. Kia returned with a bag of frozen lima beans instead. "Here, hold this over your eye. Maybe you should see a doctor, dear." She drew a soft hand gently across the opposite cheek.

"No doctor for me," declared Sam. "I'll just wait here for a few more minutes until my clothes are dry and then pick myself up and head home. I'll be fine in the morning."

"You'll do no such thing, Sam Nahoe. You're hurt, and it's still pouring outside. You'll spend the night here on that couch, and we'll see how you are in the morning."

Peggy chimed in. "Please, Daddy. It's late. Stay the night."

Sam looked over at a tuckered-out Goldie, lying clumsily on her side. "And what do you think, girl?"

His partner slowly raised herself up on all fours and padded across the room to him. He rewarded her with a belly rub, then tickled her behind the ears, eliciting a pained whine.

"She must have hurt herself in the chase," Sam said. "There's a sensitive spot behind her right ear—a tiny knot there too."

"Then you'll both spend the night here," said Kia. "That's all there is to it. Case closed."

"I guess I'm outnumbered," Sam said, the hint of a smile turning up the corners of his wide mouth.

"What about the pizza?" Peggy asked. "I'm still hungry." She snatched a slice of pepperoni from the large pie on the kitchen table, took one bite, and made a face.

"I'd forgotten all about it," said Kia. "It must be cold by now."

"It is," said Peggy. "I'll stick it in the microwave for a minute or so. That should take care of it. And you know what? There's somebody else who needs supper." She opened a cabinet door and pulled out a five-pound bag of Kibble, kept specially for Goldie's visits.

The three of them sat around the kitchen table, silent, in no mood for idle chatter. The only noise came from the dog scarfing down her food and lapping from her water bowl, three slurps at a time.

When they were finished, Kia broke the silence. "Peggy, it's 9:30 and tomorrow's a school day. Did you finish your homework?"

"Um, not quite, Mom. I still have a few math problems."

"Then go do them and get ready for bed. You can take Goldie with you to your room."

As soon as the door closed, Kia opened the linen closet and returned with an armload of bedding for the couch. Sam sat in the blue velvet wing chair that matched the couch and watched while Kia tucked in the sheets, smoothed a comforter out on top, and fluffed up the pillow. Then she leaned over and kissed him lightly on the forehead. Sam, hoping for more, placed his confident hands on her soft hips and drew her closer. But she turned and slipped away to her room, shutting the door behind her. Disappointed, Sam moved to the couch, crawled under the covers, and soon fell asleep.

He awoke a little after 2 a.m. with a sharp pain in the middle of his back that dwarfed the pain in his left eye. Shifting his body one way and then the other, he pulled one leg up and stretched the other out. Nothing seemed to work until he sat up and leaned against the back of the couch. This disruption wasn't anything new—it happened several times a week, and he'd learned to live with it. What else could he do? What he didn't expect as his eyes adjusted to the darkness was Kia seated in the wing chair. Her lovely face was grim.

"What's wrong?" he asked.

"I was worried about you. You made noises in your sleep, so I came in to see if you needed anything."

Sam patted the sofa cushion next to him, a definite invitation for her to join him. In her almost-transparent nylon nightgown, Kia slowly traversed the distance, unsure, weighing the pros and cons as she came. She sat down a foot away from him. He shifted his body closer, wrapping his right arm around her shoulders. This time his ex-wife didn't shy away. In fact, she lowered her head to rest in the crook of his sinewy neck. A minute later she turned inward and nuzzled a kiss in that same place.

He lifted her chin and planted a soft kiss on her willing lips. "I love you, sweetheart. I always will."

"I never stopped loving you, my darling," replied Kia.

"Let's get married again," said Sam.

She hesitated for only a second. "Yes!" She sprang up and pulled Sam to his feet. Arm in arm, they shuffled to her room, closing—and locking—the door behind them. Cane and Able were not needed there.

School night or not, Peggy must have been sleeping only lightly. She awoke with a start to the sound of voices in the living room and peeked out. Then, taking care to close her door silently, she hugged her friend sharing the bed.

"You see, Goldie," she whispered, "now I know that wounds, old and new, real and imagined, can and will heal, and the same is true with marriages. All it takes is two people who love and care for each other. We're going to be a family again."

The End

All this detective work makes me so doggone tired.

The Paco and Molly Mystery Series (#1)

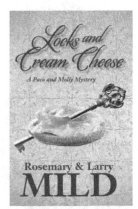

Locks and Cream Cheese—In scandal-ridden Black Rain Corners, a Chesapeake Bay mansion harbors locked rooms and deadly secrets. A wily detective and a gourmet cook tackle the case.

The Paco and Molly Mystery Series (#2)

Hot Grudge Sunday—Bank robbers and conspirators derail the sleuths' blissful honeymoon at the Grand Canyon. Can they nail the suspects after they themselves become targets?

The Paco and Molly Mystery Series (#3)

Boston Scream Pie—A teenage girl's nightmare triggers a sinister tale of twins, two feuding families, and a blonde bombshell who hates being called "Mom."

Available on Amazon.com and all e-readers.

The Dan and Rivka Sherman Mystery Series (#1)

Death Goes Postal—Rare 15th-century typesetting artifacts journey through time, leaving a horrifying imprint in their wake. Dan and Rivka risk life and limb to locate the treasures and unmask the murderer. Not quite what they expected when they bought The Olde Victorian Bookstore. (**Also available as an Amazon Audible Audiobook**.)

The Dan and Rivka Sherman Mystery Series (#2)

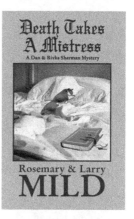

Death Takes A Mistress—A young Englishwoman is murdered by her lover. Years later, her daughter, seeking revenge, journeys from London to Annapolis, MD to find the killer and her father. But to which family does he belong? Dan and Rivka set out to expose the true villain.

The Dan and Rivka Sherman Mystery Series (#3)

Death Steals A Holy Book—Dan and Rivka inherit a rare Yiddish translation of a 14th-century holy book, but it is stolen and their book restorer is murdered. Can they recover the book and nail the culprit?

Available on Amazon.com and all e-readers.

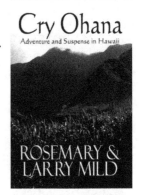

Cry Ohana, Adventure and Suspense in Hawai'i—A car accident, blackmail, and murder tear apart a Hawai'ian *'ohana* (family). Danger erupts at a Filipino wedding, a Maui resort, and the Big Island's volcanic steam vents. Can the family re-unite and bring down the killer?

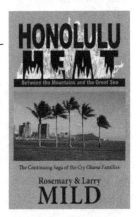

Honolulu Heat—Leilani and Alex Wong anguish over son Noah, an idealistic teenager who teeters on both sides of the law. He meets Nina Portfia, his dream girl, but they unwittingly share horrific secrets. Noah finds himself immersed in a bloody feud between a Chinatown protection racketeer and a crimeland don who, ironically, is Nina's father.

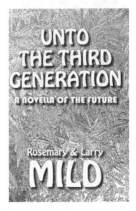

Unto the Third Generation—Two young people, each unaware of the other, volunteer to become cryonauts—physically frozen in a life-suspension experiment. Leonard, a steel worker, and Francine, a waitress, postpone their destinies for untold generations. But their lives are in jeopardy—depending upon two world-shaking events.

Available on Amazon.com and all e-readers.

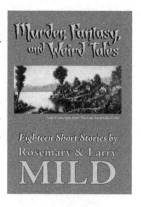

***Murder, Fantasy, and Weird Tales*—** Delve into tales of the brave, the foolhardy, and the wicked on their journeys to the unknown in Hawai'i, Japan, Cambodia, Italy, and elsewhere. Art lovers, hit women, a vampire, a lively hologram, and others reveal their secret compulsions.

***The Misadventures of Slim O. Wittz, Soft-Boiled Detective*—**"If you're looking for a truly bumbling gumshoe, you want me, Slim. I'm frequently behind the eight ball and seldom paid. In eight complete mystery stories I always bump into criminals. And you're right: my case record is remarkably shaky."

Available on Amazon.com and all e-readers.

Also by Rosemary

Miriam's World and Mine—Miriam Luby Wolfe, a junior at Syracuse U., spent her fall semester in London exploring her talents: singing, dancing, acting, and writing. But she never made it home. A terrorist bomb destroyed her plane over Lockerbie, Scotland. Learn about Miriam, the Pan Am families, the bombers, and the political fallout.

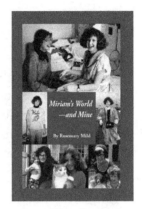

Love! Laugh! Panic! Life with My Mother—Don't we all have mixed emotions about our mothers? Rosemary Mild's mom was super-achieving, but tough to live with. Luby Pollack was a journalist, popular book author, and psychiatrist's wife. Always the heroine, and sometimes the villain, from the viewpoint of her loving but ornery daughter.

Also by Larry

No Place To Be But Here—It is not only Larry's own story, but that of his family. Join him as he tells how his two wives, three children, and five grandchildren have shaped his life as much as he has molded theirs. Tragedy is certainly no stranger as he deals with death, cancer, murder, and global terrorism, not only on the written page, but in his own life.

Available on Amazon.com and all e-readers..

182

Photograph by Craig Herndon

Rosemary and Larry Mild, cheerful partners in crime, coauthor mystery and thriller novels and short stories. Many of their wickedly entertaining stories appear in anthologies: *Dark Paradise: Mysteries in the Land of Aloha*; *Mystery in Paradise: 13 Tales of Suspense*; and *Chesapeake Crimes: Homicidal Holidays*. In 2013 the Milds waved goodbye to Severna Park, Maryland, and moved to Honolulu, Hawai'i, where they cherish time with their daughters and grandchildren.

E-mail the Milds at: roselarry@magicile.com

Visit them at: www.magicile.com

CPSIA information can be obtained
at www.ICGtesting.com
Printed in the USA
LVHW081049130819
627419LV00002B/4/P